Jane worked in the horse racing industry all her working life, now cheerily retired in the beautiful county of Dorset, living with her rescued Staffordshire Bull Terrier, Buster. She revels in sea swimming, writing, going horse racing, getting tattoos, and generally loving all the various things that the countryside has to offer.

This is her first novel.

To my father, Gilbert Southall, whom I wish I remembered.

Jane Southall

DID HER AUNT KNOW

AUSTIN MACAULEY PUBLISHERS
LONDON * CAMBRIDGE * NEW YORK * SHARJAH

Copyright © Jane Southall 2025

The right of Jane Southall to be identified as author of this work has been asserted by the author in accordance with sections 77 and 78 of the Copyright, Designs and Patents Act 1988.

All rights reserved. No part of this publication may be reproduced, stored in a retrieval system, or transmitted in any form or by any means, electronic, mechanical, photocopying, recording, or otherwise, without the prior permission of the publishers.

Any person who commits any unauthorised act in relation to this publication may be liable to criminal prosecution and civil claims for damages.

This is a work of fiction. Names, characters, businesses, places, events, locales, and incidents are either the products of the author's imagination or used in a fictitious manner. Any resemblance to actual persons, living or dead, or actual events is purely coincidental.

A CIP catalogue record for this title is available from the British Library.

ISBN 9781035879175 (Paperback)
ISBN 9781035879182 (ePub e-book)

www.austinmacauley.com

First Published 2025
Austin Macauley Publishers Ltd®
1 Canada Square
Canary Wharf
London
E14 5AA

Thanks to Catherine Cosby for her endless patience and sense of humour.

Be the woman you want to be.

The story begins in a rural village in the Warwickshire countryside one gloomy November Thursday evening—sometime between World War I and World War II.

1

Ida Mumford, a slim dark-haired child, started to shiver as the tepid bath water rapidly cooled. She snatched her knees up to her body, clasping her thin arms around her legs. Her tears, in a steady procession, ran off the bottom of her chin to join the now-cold water. She began to howl, sobbing heart-wrenching gasps of tears and snot.

The child, now shaking violently with fear and chill, stood up and, wobbling as she did so, held onto the side of the bath. She then put one foot onto the stone floor followed by the other foot onto the floor. She promptly sat down and wailed as if her throat would split apart.

Maude, whilst concentrating on stirring the freshly chopped potatoes into the stew pot, thought she heard the sound of an injured animal. Having lived in the same village all her life, she was well-accustomed to the various winter evening countryside sounds. Adding carrots and leeks to her thickening venison stew, Maude heard the noise again, louder and clearer this time. Putting down her wooden spoon, she listened earnestly. Easily recognisable this time as a child's cry.

Maude hurriedly took off her apron and pulled the stew pot to the cooler side of the range. She rushed out of her back door, pushing through the privet hedge to her left, and put her shoulder to her sister's back door which she knew was always jammed in the damp winter months. The door lurched open dramatically. There, huddled on the blue lias stone floor was her three-year-old niece. Gathering two threadbare woollen blankets from the back of a chair, Maude wrapped Ida up in them.

She then picked her up and sat on one of the two rickety wooden kitchen chairs, comforting Ida at the same time as attempting to dry her as best as she could. Maude shouted, 'Sylvie, are you here?'

There was no response.

Shouting again, this time louder still, but no response; at the same time aware that Sylvie's green bag was not in its usual place on a hook on the kitchen wall.

Maude quietly asked the damp bundle on her lap, 'Where's Mummy?' At first, getting no response, she quietly asked the question again.

Ida whispered, 'Mummy not here.'

It was now gone six, the evening foggy as it sometimes was in November. Maude sat up and carried the child up the steep uneven wooden stairs. Going into the smaller of the two upstairs rooms, she gathered some clothes together from those that were strewn about the floor. Dressing Ida in a green dress, long brown socks, black leather boots and two very worn-out-looking woollen pullovers. Then she stuffed what other clothes she could find under her free arm and with Ida on her hip went back downstairs, turning off the kitchen overhead light and pushing back through the privet hedge and back into her own welcoming warm kitchen.

Elmer sat at the kitchen table reading the football results in the *Birmingham Gazette*. 'Where have you been, Maudie? I thought you had left me high and dry! What's with the little'un?'

Raising her eyebrows, Maude replied, 'Sylvie's nowhere to be seen; her purse gone; don't know about clothes. This one, bless her, left in the tin bath…poor little bean.'

Elmer said, 'Get some hot food in us all, Maudie; little'un will feel a lot better for it.' Stew devoured, Ida sitting happily between her aunt and Elmer, sipping at a mug of milk her eyelids flickering with tiredness.

'That sister of yours…what next?' muttered Elmer crossly.

'Not in front of the bean,' Maude said sharply back at him. She settled Ida warmly upstairs in the box room, under one of Maude's handmade quilts.

Elmer puffed away rhythmically on his pipe. 'That Sylvie, she has gone too far this time round. Did she say anything to you this morning?'

'No,' said Maude. 'I saw her briefly when I went to get logs in. She was standing by the kitchen window looking at a piece of paper. Then I went off to work, not seen her since.'

Elmer looked at her and said, 'You better be asking out and about tomorrow if anyone has seen her or knows anything. What are you going to do with Ida? Can't take her to work, can you?'

A very tired and worried Maude said, 'Let's sleep on it now. Maybe Sylvie will be back in the morning.'

The fog had finally lifted, leaving a still clear winter day. Elmer, up at dawn and put the kettle on the range to make his flask of tea. Loaded the stove with coal, packed a tin with cheese sandwiches, which Maude had readied the night before, into his canvas bag and shouted up the stairway, 'Maudie, sort that sister of yours out, it's not right,' before setting off to the forge to set his apprentice straight for the busy day ahead.

2

Maude was dressing slowly, as she heard the back door clink shut and Elmer stride away in his heavy work boots. She was quiet; hoping the child in the next-door room would sleep late, giving her time to think through the last few days. Had Sylvie given any indication that she was planning to leave? No, she had not, but Sylvie was a law unto herself and well-known in the village and surrounding areas for being "a bit different" and rustically seductive to the local men from an early teenager.

Now, at twenty-two, being five years younger than Maude, she was a striking dark brown-haired woman with mesmerising green eyes, which had the ability to penetrate the very psyche of whoever she spoke to be it Mrs Bryan who ran the bakery or her brother-in-law's apprentice Davy. The identity of Ida's father was greatly speculated upon but with no candidate the clear winner. Sylvie utterly refused to cooperate or add any snippet of a clue to the momentum of gathering gossip.

Having lost their mother in childhood, Maude and Ida were left somewhat adrift after her death from tuberculosis. James Mumford, their small acreage tenant farmer and horse breeder father, was ill-equipped to deal with his two young daughters, preferring to spend his time at the races or Perry Barr greyhound track.

Maude had been caught up in Sylvie's web of denial throughout the early months of her pregnancy. When she began to irretrievably show through her clothing, Maude was ashamed beyond belief. The sisters had no older female relatives to comfort or counsel them. Sylvie, seemingly unbothered by the alarming tightening of her waistband, cheerfully continued with her work as a shop assistant in Steynings, the saddlery shop in nearby Upton Wootton. Smiling at customers and beguiling the predominantly male clientele on a daily basis.

Maude laid out the freshly prepared porridge and honey into two bowls on the kitchen table, along with a piping hot mug of tea for herself before finally gently waking Ida and dressing her.

The child, despite knowing her aunt well, sat silently, gently spooning the creamy porridge at slow intervals into her mouth. It occurred to Maude, as she watched her intently, was Ida thinking through yesterday's events in her mind? But of course, that was nonsense, Maude realised. Ida was only her very young niece.

What to do? Maude muttered to herself. She was due at Mrs Noble's in an hour at 8:30 in readiness for a day of alterations, machining and dressmaking. *A dressmaker was not the ideal nursery, but a whole lot better than a blacksmith's forge*, she thought, smiling to herself. Thoroughly aware that this was no smiling situation.

Mrs Noble could be tricky on the smoothest of days in the workshop. She really had no choice but to set off a bit early now and call on Janice, Sylvie's closest friend who lived above Barclays's, the butcher's shop. Maybe, after talking to Janice she could stop fretting.

Somehow Maude was going to have to make a makeshift seat for her niece in the basket on the front of her bicycle. But not before popping back to Sylvie's place and scouting around for any clues as to her whereabouts. Popping Ida on her hip, Maude retraced her steps of the previous evening back into Sylvie's rented cottage. Up the stairs and into her sister's bedroom. On opening the small wardrobe, she saw that Sylvie's clothes were gone, along with the few bits and pieces from the bedroom table.

On the bedside shelf, there was a copy of the previous Thursday's *Coventry Evening News*. Opening the paper and carefully turning the pages in the hope of finding some sort of pointer resulted in Maude letting the newspaper fall to the dusty wooden floor. It revealed absolutely nothing at all.

Conscious of not wanting to turn up at work late, and with an unexpected childminding situation to explain, Maude hurried to her bicycle where she padded out the basket with an old coat of hers and a cushion, before buttoning up Ida's coat, pulling her bobble hat down over her ears and then popping her into the basket. This brought chortles of delight to the little girl.

Off they set, first towards Marshcombe and Janice. Roy Barclay, red-faced and whiskery in every crevice of his sixty-one-year-old face, said sternly that Janice was "out back". Maude and Ida found Janice folding clean blue and white striped butcher aprons. 'Hello, Maudie, what you doing visiting me? Shouldn't you be at work? And what's with little Ida?' she said, bending down and scooping Ida up onto her shoulders.

'You seen our Sylvie? She's gone, seems to have left home and taken all her clothes. Left the little bean abandoned in a cold bath yesterday evening.'

'No! Never! Poor little poppet. I saw her last Saturday with Ida in Gorringe's chatting to Sara, seemed her normal mischievous self, laughing and sassing with Mr Gorringe.'

'Thanks, Janice, I have got to get to work, promise me if you see her or hear anything, you will let me know, promise me now.'

'I promise, Maudie,' said Janice as she let Ida gently back down to the floor.

Maude cycled hard and fast to get to Mrs Noble's. Leaving her bicycle in the lean-to shed. She went into the small workshop, where Anna the younger girl, who had not long started work there, was already unpicking a green dress. Mrs Noble, or Mrs N to her employees, saw Maude with her niece and straightening herself up to her full and commanding five foot ten inches tall said, 'Maude, who do we have here? Isn't that Sylvie's girl?'

'Oh, Mrs N, yes, this is my niece, Ida. My sister Sylvie's little girl. I am looking after her. Sylvie seems to have gone away.' At this point, Ida pulled her hand out of Maude's and slowly sank to the floor, attracted by a stray reel of red cotton on the floor and began spinning it.

'Well, how long will she be gone for?'

'I have no idea, but she has no one else to mind her Mrs N.'

Beginning to tire of this unusual start to the working day Mrs Noble shrugged and responded sharply, 'Well, the child can stay in here with you and Anna, but I don't want her in my sewing room and no wailing or bawling. You better get busy sharpish in your off time in finding that tricksy sister of yours.'

The day passed reasonably smoothly. Ida was clearly in the habit of entertaining herself to a greater degree. Which came as no surprise, as Sylvie hardly fell into the ideal mother category.

Bob Dewey was less than pleased when Maude showed up at the saddlers just as he was about to shut up the shop. As she expected, Bob had not heard from Sylvie; not turning up for work for him was a dismissal offence. His wife was also disgruntled and that was only because Sylvie was such a good saleswoman, if a fella came in for one set of reins, he invariably left with two sets. As she minded Ida cycling home, Maude realised that the general lack of sympathy and concern for Sylvie stemmed from her impudent and misguided behaviour since childhood.

3

Elmer sat down in the carver chair at the end of the kitchen table and watched Ida play with a woollen stuffed elephant that Maude had made her the previous Christmas.

'What's to, Maudie? It is not right for your sister to take off, and you landed with the small one. I am going down the Blue Boar for a stout after my grub. See if any of the lads from Durent's racing stables have heard anything. They love to talk about everyone else's business.'

With that, Maude dished up the cold ham and mashed potatoes and her runner bean pickle and the three of them ate their tea with Ida listlessly poking at the mash.

The following morning, after Elmer's trip to the pub, had drawn a blank. His enquiries had only yielded laughter and a chorus of 'Well, that is no surprise!' from his fellow drinkers. After seeing Elmer off to the forge with a packed lunch, she set her mind to go over and visit her father on Saturday afternoon.

James Mumford was lugging two bales of hay into Lower Ground field, to feed that year's spring lambs. He enjoyed his Romney sheep and a few Hereford cattle. But his heart lay with his horses, since as a boy, helping with the plough horses, he had developed a deep affinity with them. He had bred a couple of winners, not big race winners just provincial egg and spoon track triumphs. Since Margaret had died, his horses had been his saving grace.

Sylvie had a way with the horses, but she was always a little bit too impatient, as was her inclination. He liked that she worked well at Steynings, and they were good to take her on again after "the trouble". Particularly, Helen Dewey was seeing Ida during working hours.

James had been at a loss not only when the girls' mother died but as much so when Sylvie announced one Sunday that she was going to have a baby. He had hit the whisky hard that night. Slumped over he had muttered, 'Margaret what am I to do? You would have known.' Ida loved her grandfather but saw him infrequently, usually when her mother wanted some cash to help her get by with the rent.

The hay shaken out for the sheep, James headed back to the yard just as Maude appeared on her bicycle with his granddaughter perched and smiling widely on the front of it. 'Hello, Father, look who I have with me!'

'Granda,' Ida chirped.

'Well, this is a very nice surprise. Sylvie not well?'

'Let's get the kettle on Da, and you and I can have a chat.' Maude made the tea whilst tidying up the kitchen. Ida sitting on the window seat with Buster, the all-knowing tri-coloured Staffordshire Bull Terrier, who loved nothing better than a good ear rub.

James Mumford said seriously, 'C'mon Maudie what's going on?' Maude, sipping her mug of sweet tea, explained to her stunned father that Sylvie had disappeared four days ago, with no sightings of her—nothing. She continued telling him the whole sorry story so far as she knew it.

James sat with his head in his hands, quiet and breathing heavily before eventually saying, 'Was there anything in that Coventry newspaper you found, any clues at all?'

'No, nothing that I could see Da, Janice knew nothing either. Bob Dewey, has already replaced her at Steynings.'

James, not a man of many words at the best of times suggested, 'Maudie, how about you putting a notice in the *Coventry Evening News* for our Sylvie to get in contact and with a picture to see if anyone knows her whereabouts?'

'That is a plan, Da, I will do that next week, come on let us take Ida out to see the horses.'

Ida seemed content enough, as far as Maude could judge. Not being a mother, she and Elmer had so far been unable to have children. Elmer, twelve years older than her. Very much a "safe bet" her father would say as a husband. Highly skilled in his trade and hard working. Maude had always liked him, often when she was young accompanying James to the forge when one of his horses was due to be shod.

Sylvie and Maude were vastly different characters. It was as though they hailed from totally opposite backgrounds and nurturing, never sharing any mutual values. Maude was always the homemaker, running shy of any form of confrontation, always seeking harmony and order. So very different too in physique to her younger sister. Barely five feet two inches tall and not in possession of the glossy dark brown locks that Sylvie had but blessed with wispy sable ferret-coloured hair and small, glassy pale blue eyes.

Sylvie, however, seemed to have an almost pathological desire for stimulation. Thriving on disorder and jeopardy at every turn. Early on, she had an abundance of confidence, it was clear to most who knew her that her life was not going to tread a path of socially acceptable and predictive norms.

Insisting at thirteen on riding a bicycle on three-inch ice, shrieking with joy as she slid alarmingly sideways into a frozen ditch, rendering her upside down with the bicycle on top of her. Emerging she claimed, 'Told you I could do it.'

Disappointingly, but not unsurprisingly, the notice in the *Coventry Evening News*, two weeks to the day Sylvie vanished, reaped no news.

Meanwhile, Mrs Noble had no choice but to let Maude bring Ida to work. She was well aware, that Maude would be very hard to replace as she was a superb seamstress. Janice mentioned to Maude that Sylvie had briefly talked of a man who had come to Steynings one day some months ago, buying a tweed cap. Sylvie remarked with a big smirk and a slow wink, 'He was a proper sort, lived in Birmingham.'

With so little information, Maude vowed to herself to ensure that Ida was secure and happy. The cheerful child often asked where her mother was, eliciting, 'Your mother had to go to see a friend,' from Maude, on an almost daily basis.

Elmer, tired though he was when he got back from a long day shoeing the local horses, some often not particularly cooperative in having a fresh set of steel shoes nailed on, always had the necessary energy to play and entertain Ida. Often playing with the wooden farmstead that he had as a Christmas gift as a boy. After finishing the last horse, his apprentice Davy and he would make up the shoes needed for the next day's equine customers. Be it a child's pony, heavy horses or a racehorse or two from Durent's.

He, like the Mumford family, had lived in the area all his life. Never felt the need to venture much further than

Birmingham or Worcester. His father had died in a tree-felling accident when Elmer was nineteen. His mother, crushed by grief and depression, moved to Tewkesbury to live with her older sister. By this time, Elmer was thriving in his farrier training under Rob Woods whose byword was "steady away gets the task done".

4

As the weeks expanded into months, Maude was gratefully aware that the speculative village chitter-chatter regarding Sylvie's disappearance was starting to subside. Apart from Mrs Noble, whose demeanour bore the resemblance of an irritated penguin. Asking almost daily, 'Any news, Maude, on the wanderer?'

James Mumford, his farm chores completed for the day, pulled on his big heavy brown racing coat. Which was equipped with a secure inside breast pocket to safely stash away cash, that he might be wily enough to win at the greyhound racing that afternoon. Buster gave him a knowing sideways look, accustomed to being left on his old sheepskin rug when the racing coat was donned.

Kipper Brown appeared in the yard in his battered Commer truck, pressed the sad-sounding horn and James swung himself into the passenger side. Kipper was known to everyone as Kipper, but nobody knew why, not even Kipper. Unmarried, almost lanky, with unfortunately vast red ears. He was some might say, if they were feeling uncharitable, that Kipper was a "dodge pot" who did a bit of everything, mostly haulage in his truck.

The two men after mutual pleasantries, travelled the first few miles in silence as men who know each other well. Until, Kipper said, 'Any news on your Sylvie?'

After what seemed to Kipper like a long wait, James finally said, 'Not a word, Kip. I don't know what to think, to be honest. I am trying not to think. You know from the get-go, our Sylvie girl, was always going to walk the wrong path in this life. Just hoping that she is safe, and thankful daily that her mother is not here to see it.' Silence refilled the cab.

The two men stopped at the Blue Boar for a swift pint and pickled eggs. Being a Saturday lunchtime, the bar was busy, with several lads who worked at Durent's racing yard, some two miles away. There was much nudging and smirking and sideways looks from the boys, some already steaming into their weekly wage, as Kipper and James approached the bar to buy their pints.

'Found your slippin' Sylvie yet?' one of the bigger lads ventured to a chorus of raucous laughter from the others.

Kipper sensed the anger rising in James, 'C'mon leave them, they have had plenty too many pints.' He said hurriedly pushing his friend to the far end of the bar.

Back in the vehicle, Kipper ventured, 'You been to the police station about Sylvie?'

Sighing, James said, 'Our Maude went over to see Brian Dawson the day after Sylvie left. You know what a lazy jack he is, just doing as little as possible up in his police cottage until he retires. No good to man nor beast. He said Sylvie had probably joined the circus! Calls himself a copper, he wouldn't spot a crime before his very eyes' bloody useless idiot.'

Perry Barr Greyhound Stadium was alive with jostling, cheerful punters, intent on having a good Saturday afternoon at "the dogs". Kipper and James knew a few trainers, who always put them onto a "good thing" when the price was right. But on this particular afternoon, there was only one dog running trained by their friend Barnes O'Shea, who trained about twenty greyhounds over near Coleshill.

When Barnes fancied a runner of his, he would indicate this to his two friends by feigning blowing his nose as he put the expected winner into the traps. Of course, this was not a fool proof procedure, should Barnes be suffering from a heavy winter cold. But invariably it was successful on most occasions, as both Kipper and James knew the greyhound game well enough. As Back Chat Bob was loaded into the No. 2 trap by Barnes, he pulled a grubby grey handkerchief out of his cord trouser pocket and appeared to blow his nose. Pleasingly, Back Chat Bob broke fast from his trap, cornered well at the first bend and was still in command going over the line. Leaving Kipper and James a couple of quid apiece better off than when they had left the Blue Boar.

5

The weeks faded into months. Spring came bringing boisterous life to the village, and easier living to the hardworking country dwellers. Maude was a regular at Police Constable Brian Dawson's small police office at the side of his house. His general response to her enquiries was thoroughly unenthusiastic, to say the least.

Dawson, whilst devouring a very large slice of fruit cake, greeted Maude with a languid, 'Oh, it's you again. No news here, Maude. I've sent telegrams to the Coventry and Birmingham police stations. No women's bodies in the canals!' Then he turned back to his cake and mug of tea. His wife was a prolific baker, and he didn't like to disappoint her!

Ida continued to spend her weekdays in Mrs Noble's workshop. Drawing in a notebook that Janice had given her. She continued to ask about her mother, but over the months this became less frequent. The child had an air of self-containment. She ate happily and slept reasonably well, but washing began to become increasingly stressful.

Maude, ill-equipped to deal with the anxious little Ida, did her best to reassure her and distract her with a timely bribe of a visit to Granda to see the horses. Despite being anxious, Ida had her mother's inner shrewdness and Maude's bribery had to get more creative as weekly bath days went by. Trips to Dixon Cakes and the sweetshop became regular additional bath time incentives.

Elmer worked extremely hard, five and a half days a week. He did not lack drive or determination, but what he did not have in abundance was emotional intelligence. Happy as he was to engage with Ida on a nominal level after work and on Sundays, he struggled to support his beloved Maudie other than in practical ways. After several months, Elmer was resigned to the fact that they would most likely be de facto parents to Ida. He told Maude he would do the absolute best he could.

6

Major Taylor, the landlord of Sylvie's rented cottage, was quick to re-let it. The Dunne family moved in, Katriona and Paul, with their almost six-year-old son Jonjo. Paul, a hardy perennial of an Irish Kilkenny man through and through. Kat, as she preferred to be called, was a Dublin girl. Paul was the latest addition of reinforced steel "jump" jockeys, attached to Durent's increasingly successful racing yard.

They were a cheerful trio and Maude was grateful for the refreshing outlook and humour that Kat radiated. Paul was often away overnight if the race meeting; he was riding at was a metropolitan track other than Birmingham. Maude, ever the thoughtful individual, was always quick to check in on Kat and the cheeky Jonjo if they were on their own. Offering helpful suggestions regarding shopping and work opportunities. Kat had trained as a nurse in Dublin before she had been charmed by Paul's masterly seduction offensive after meeting him at Punchestown races one bright April day.

Little Jonjo was an able and enthusiastic entertainer for Ida, for which Maude was eternally grateful.

7

On Forde Street in Birmingham, the weak autumn sun filtered into the Divine Emporium as Eunice pulled up the blinds. She then set about arranging the delphiniums that she had bought on her way to the shop that morning. Always taking time to be creative and to make an attractive centrepiece on the oak table in the middle of the showroom.

The shop, which was spacious and airy, gave the impression of a rather grandiose luxury dress shop. With two large three-seater velvet chaise lounges and gilt mirrors which flanked the cream walls on either side of the high-end dresses and gowns. Wooden elm floors were dressed with a number of Persian rugs. The overall ambience was destined to encourage customers to relax and "dig deep" as Eunice was heard to say at least once a day to her assistants. Upstairs there was a basic kitchen and bathroom, a sitting room and five other rooms, all thoughtfully and charmingly decorated.

Promptly at ten o'clock Peggy, Dina, Lucy, and Martha bustled in through the showroom door all at once and in a flurry of chatter, the clatter of heels and a perfumed haze greeted Eunice with a chirpy chorus of "Morning".

Eunice replied, 'Good morning, girls. Right, let us get ready for a hopefully busy Saturday ahead.'

Dina was the eldest of the quartet and the most experienced, having worked at Divine for five years. Lucy, a quick-witted tall girl who was prone to one of Eunice's pet hates, back chat.

Peggy, a naturally petite blonde and almost delicate in her looks, had only recently joined the team some ten months ago, but she was quick on the uptake and good at closing a sale. Then there was Martha, funny, sarcastic, and equipped with the sharpest of tongues delivered in a strong Scot's accent.

At the dot of eleven o'clock, the showroom door swung open and with a flourish in swept Eunice's mother, Marjorie Peyton who was not only the owner but self-proclaimed Grande Dame of Forde Street. Dressed from head to toe in pale violet with wrists, neck and fingers glistening and twinkling with what was certainly not inexpensive jewellery. Marjorie Peyton was accompanied everywhere by Pico, her rather spoilt, overweight, and bad-tempered black pug, who sported a white leather embossed collar with matching lead.

The girls, including Eunice, were expected to line up, each and every day, on Marjorie's arrival for inspection. Perfect make-up, hair, attire and nails were the expected high standard of the matriarch. Nothing less would do, the girls, all intent on doing well for themselves, were happy to conform.

Marjorie would then have a chat with each of them individually, clarifying what was expected of them and which customers might be anticipated on that day. Once she was satisfied, she would retire upstairs to the beautifully decorated sitting room and drink tea at her ornate ormolu desk and read the *Birmingham Echo* and the French fashion magazines, that she received in the post monthly.

Mr Peyton had been the unfortunate victim of a tram accident, dying instantaneously when Eunice was fourteen months old. This family tragedy had as much effect on Marjorie as if she had laddered an old pair of stockings! George Peyton, an accountant, had been a necessity as far as Marjorie had been concerned. She hailed from humble beginnings in Walsall. Having met George in a cinema queue, she unashamedly and politely persecuted him until he was pussy-whipped into submission. It had crossed the tongues of her closest friends, that she may even have had a clairvoyant moment regarding the tram accident!

Armed with her dead husband's life insurance and comfortably homed, Marjorie had set about her life's ambition to open a luxury dress shop in Birmingham. From a young age, she had walked to school mulling over various names she might call her business. Finally settling on Divine at about sixteen years of age. The sheer pride and jubilation that surged through her when the sign writer finished the striking Bellochero font above the doorway, was a moment she savoured.

8

Eunice, every bit her mother's daughter, was driven, avaricious and single-minded and shared Marjorie's talent for the "gift of the gab" and command of any situation.

In looks, she was not any great likeness to her mother who was tall and long-limbed. Eunice was of average height and had attractive even features, with almost fern green eyes, wavy auburn hair and generous lips. From a young age, she had loved clothes, parading up and down their tiled hallway in her mother's monk-strap, Continental-heeled shoes. Much to Marjorie's encouragement and entertainment, Eunice strutted whilst simultaneously swishing her hair and skirt. She worked hard at school and made friends easily. By the time she was three, Divine Gowns had been created and owing to her mother's almost zealous passion for ensuring that the emporium on Forde Street was a roaring success, a nanny was employed.

Dorothy arrived each morning at eight just as Marjorie was applying the finishing touches to her handsome face, before leaving for the shop and not returning until eight in the evening. By this time, Eunice was tired and happily tucked up in bed. Her day with Dorothy was so stimulating and fun that she did not miss her mother. On Sundays, Marjorie would dedicate her time entirely to her daughter, sometimes a walk in the park or a good lunch at the Grand Hotel.

Dorothy, or Dotty as Eunice called her, enjoyed her job, and loved enriching her small charge's day. As Divine Gowns became increasingly successful, Dorothy would stay over, only going home to her family in Kings Heath on Sundays. As the years went by, her role became more of a housekeeper than a nanny. Which suited her skills well, being efficient and with a splendid sense of humour. It surprised her that Marjorie, being the striking woman that she was, never had a male suitor after being widowed.

By the time Eunice had started in school, it had dawned on Dorothy that Marjorie had little respect for men in general, referring to them as "gulls" her word for puppets. "Gulls" were easily manipulated and unchallenging marks. She had overheard Marjorie talking to Dina when she called at the house one day saying, 'Dina girl, I have said it before, and I will say it again; men, just feed them and fuck them.' Dorothy had been in Marjorie's employment long enough not to be shocked. This brief snippet of overheard conversation would stand her in good stead when she eventually married her long-time suitor, Brian.

9

Eunice oversaw a strict regime at the gown shop. The girls each took it in turns to make tea and run errands for Marjorie to the post office, florist, chemist, or cake shop. They also cleaned the shop including the upstairs rooms and paid particular attention to the side entrance, down an alleyway that led to a smart and solid dark blue door with a cast iron knocker in the shape of a flower head.

Whichever of the girls was on the lunch run would be given the necessary cash by Marjorie and returned with a selection of freshly made sandwiches and fresh fruit. Fruit, the matriarch insisted helped the girls' complexion stay clear and healthy. Absolutely no food was allowed in the showroom. It had to be eaten in the kitchen upstairs at the linen bedecked table. Divine not only sold beautiful evening and day wear, but also the finest silk hosiery: stockings in three colours, Champagne, French tan and white, girdles, fancy garters, and silk slips all lay displayed in armoires on pale pink tissue paper.

The two dressing rooms, as the changing rooms were called, were spacious with pale blue velvet-covered chairs in the corner of each one and discreetly shielding the customer were heavy cream velvet drapes held back, when not in use, by elaborate gold tiebacks. The customers admired their potential "Divine" purchase in six-foot-high ornate mirrors.

Behind the highly polished maple wood serving counter, there were four gilt-backed stools each upholstered in yet more blue velvet. The girls were allowed to rest on these but only when the store was devoid of customers. At either end of the long counter, there were always two large seasonal flower arrangements. During the winter months, Eunice would have a large display of dried hydrangeas.

Display cabinets behind the serving area housed kid, leather, silk, and fur-lined gloves. Marjorie had her own line of lingerie which was made for her in Leeds. All the girls wore Divine lingerie, and it was a strong seller. When Dina was selling a set to a younger customer, she could be overheard saying outside one of the dressing rooms with a grin, 'This set will catch you a bedroom buccaneer.'

It was a happy place to work, each of the girls played to their strengths. Eunice was particularly good at dealing with the few men who came in with some perhaps putting cash behind the counter for his "niece" when she next came to treat herself. There was, of course, Donald, forty-something, medium height and with what was left of his gossamer-like fair hair, almost bald. A monthly regular who liked nothing better than to treat himself to a beautiful tea dress. He was incredibly popular with the girls, enjoying a joke and often bringing them cream cakes or chocolates.

Marjorie and Donald were old friends, and for him, she obligingly closed the shop for half an hour the last Thursday in the month thus ensuring that he could shop in peace and enjoy himself, a splendid highlight to his otherwise quiet, repetitive life.

Lucy had a flair for dealing with some of the older women who shopped there. Just knowing when to upsell and delight in knowing that the customer had left with three dresses when they had had every intention of buying "just the one dear"!

Martha specialised in alterations, pinning and chalk marking the various gowns, so they would fit the customer just perfectly. She did not, of course, make the adjustments herself. These would be done by Elsie, a retired tailor's assistant who collected the alterations once a week.

10

As the months passed, niece and aunt inevitably grew close. Maude always sensed a predisposition in Ida to self-containment and an alarming confidence for one so young. She recognised these traits as an absolute replica of Sylvie's character. Not a day went by without her fretfully being disquieted over her sister's disappearance, but also she constantly reassured herself that her sister was safe and happy somewhere.

Despite their country upbringing, Sylvie had always "been other" as Mrs Noble had once bizarrely said. The bright city lights were going to be for Sylvie, as strong a lure as for a greyhound chasing a hare around the track. If she had been born in a hospital, Maude would have thought her sister had been swapped at birth.

Ida seemed to enjoy her hours at Mrs Noble's, spending them drawing at a little table that had been set up for her at the back of the workshop. She also appeared to love the small scraps of hem or discarded cuffs that were cast into the "snips basket", twisting and tying the bits of material together. For all the outward appearances, this little girl was thriving, and this reassured Maude that she was doing something right in bringing up her abandoned niece.

Elmer metronomically went to work every day with the occasional evening pint or three at the Blue Boar saying to Maude, whilst putting on his jacket as he left after his tea, 'Just to keep up with the doings out there in the world,' and with that, he went down the lane sucking hard on his pipe.

If he was honest with himself, and he could not be anything but, he was secretly pleased that Sylvie had performed her moonlit flit. He had groaned to himself that day when he had heard from his beloved Maude that her sister was moving in next door. Being in his sister-in-law's company had always unnerved him. For sure, he was not particularly worldly wise or experienced with women, but he forever felt horrors around her. It was after she lifted her camisole over her head, baring her perfectly formed breasts topped with hazelnut nipples at her bedroom window when he was walking up the garden path one summer's evening that he had decided to do almost anything to try and avoid her completely. He had looked away immediately, his heart charging about in his chest, and with a letterbox red face had turned on his heels and retreated back to the Blue Boar.

11

The workforce at Durent's was predominantly male, mostly Midlanders, a few lads from Malton, four from Ireland and not including the newly arrived Paul. The majority lived in the yard, catered for by the eternally talkative and widowed Mrs Neave or "Neavsey" as the boys affectionately called her. She was an amalgam of cook, counsellor, and general keeper of the peace. When the majority of the lads' wages had been profligated in the local pubs, fights were prone to break out, but Mrs Neave would soon have the situation under control and some sort of harmony restored.

Three of the lads, Pecker, so called because of his large nose, Danny and Steve had all been in the running potentially as Ida's father. With Steve being the odds-on favourite candidate. The only evidence, which was shaky at best, was the observation of Sylvie having a lengthy conversation with him as he collected some repaired racing saddles from Steynings. The three paternal suspects were not in the least perturbed by the rumour factory that abounded at the time. Amongst the racing world, it only enhanced the lads standing and consequently, they wore the accusation as a badge of pride and amusement.

12

James Mumford had by now resigned himself to the sad fact that most likely Sylvie might not come back. The tittle-tattling and muttering, as he entered the pub, had now thankfully ceased. He had been through the same treatment back before Ida was born. However, this time around it all just added to his feeling of inadequacy where his youngest daughter was concerned, but she was an adult and a defiant and self-willed one at that.

Maude and Ida would visit the small farm about twice a month. Whilst Maude would busy herself with some household chores for her father, James would take Ida out and about the fields and barns tending to his horses and livestock which she loved, all the time asking questions and being as confident around the animals as her mother had been at the same age. The familial trait was not lost on James. He was relieved and happy to see that there were no outward signs of distress or trauma in his granddaughter, and this at least brought him some comfort.

13

As the seasons changed, the lives of Sylvie's family continued unabated, driven by the necessity of paying the rent and having some degree of contentment and fulfilment in their lives. Ida thrived in all aspects of her life. She was coming to look on Maude and Elmer as her parents, and they on her as their long-wanted child.

She spent many an hour kicking a ball about the back garden with Jonjo, and often being confident enough to go next door to ask him to come "play out". He taught her to ride his bicycle, initially with him holding the saddle running alongside, with the tips of her toes on the pedals. This scene brought the most vivid memories lurching back to Maude of her sister crashing into the ditch after performing her "ice cycling" act.

In the main, Maude tried to stop the painful angst-inducing thoughts of her sister's sudden and complete disappearance. What plagued her mind most was why on earth would Sylvie put little Ida in a bath and then proceed to turn her back on her life. Maude was sure as she could be that her sister had not been forcefully taken from her cottage on that foggy November evening. But as she sat at her sewing machine under the beady eye of Mrs Noble, she would find herself muttering, 'Why, oh why leave the bean in the tub?'

Ida relished school; she was a bright girl with an inquiring mind who made friends easily and was as happy playing with the boys as with the girls. She had a knack for making all the adults laugh which endeared her to just about everybody.

Often, she would pop in to see Janice at the butcher's on her way home from school and ask for a chunky marrow bone to give to her granda's faithful and stubborn dog, Buster. If Roy Barclay was not looking, Janice would slip Ida a couple of pork chops wrapped in brown paper to take home for Maude and Elmer. Ida was capable of lighting up any room anywhere that she was present; she seemed to radiate joy and an enviable enthusiasm for life. This part of her personality Maude recognised as her sister's genes, but the ability to create laughter—who knew maybe a paternal trait?

Maude was delighted to find that Ida showed an interest in her general appearance and what she wore despite her rumbustious tom-boy tendencies—cycling and swimming in the big lake at the back of Lord Teversham's vast estate, with Jonjo and his classmates. Ida was confident enough to duck them and boisterously instigated games of swim-tag. Of course, this glee-packed swimming was not permitted by the Teversham's Estate Manager, so it was Ida who was dispatched over the estate's stone wall to see if the coast was clear, before whistling to the others indicating that some swim time beckoned. There was many a time that Owen Butters, Lord Teversham's Game Keeper had chased them from the lake bellowing, 'You little tykes, get gone with the lot of you.'

After Sylvie's abandonment of her daughter, Maude was only too happy to see her niece irrepressibly joyous and gladdened by life.

In the school holidays, Ida also had begun to help out at Mrs Noble's, unpicking hems and cuffs, sewing buttons, making tea, sweeping up, and generally making herself useful about the workshop. Having been going there with Maude from such a young age, these small tasks were second nature to her.

14

Three times a year, in first-class comfort, Marjorie would relinquish her unyielding grip on the shop and take the train from Birmingham New Street station down to London. These trips were taken in order to buy stock for the shop; staying in a splendidly plush hotel she would say on her return home. Her stay, never more than four nights, would include taking in a show. Two of her favourites were The Gypsy Princess at the Prince of Wales theatre and the Rebel Maid at the Empire. She preferred Dress Circle seats and would often sit in her allotted seat for some time after the show's cast had taken their final encore just soaking up the ambience. Marjorie never worried about the conventional social norms of "going about" unaccompanied as she always alluded to her imaginary brother Richard who had let her down yet again.

Before returning to Birmingham, an indulgent visit to her best-loved store Fortnum & Mason was made, so she could buy a selection of macarons and strawberry whip tartlets for Eunice and the girls. That said, Marjorie did adore the coffee-flavoured macaroons and often ate several of these on the train journey home.

It was not lost on her that it was her staff who helped make Divine Emporium what it was. Of course, the beautiful clothes she stocked sang for themselves, but her customers thoroughly appreciated the service they received there, often remarking on this fact to Marjorie if she saw them out and about in Birmingham.

Many a time, when visiting London on buying trips, Marjorie would mull over the thought of opening a store in London, but this idea never became more than just a thought. In the Midlands, she knew her market inside and out and had perfected her retailing skills superbly. Occasionally on the return trip, she would allow herself a brief, self-congratulatory daydream in which she applauded the young Marjorie for just how far she had come.

Meanwhile, back in Birmingham, whilst Marjorie shopped, sourced stock and took in a show or two in London, Eunice and her well-practised team of girls held the fort. Eunice always enjoyed the challenge of endeavouring to increase the takings whilst her mother was away and Lucy, Dina, Martha, and Peggy's mouths watering at the thought of the Mayfair macarons and fancies in a smart pink box that would surely accompany Marjorie on her return to Divine; of course, minus the coffee ones that she had snaffled on the train.

During the journey home, Marjorie relaxed and relished one of her most enjoyable pastimes people-watching. This was something that she had done from an early age when she was lurking about in the city's gardens whilst her mother was at work. As an adult, she liked to think that she could discover an enormous amount about a person by studying them, even from some distance. She was fascinated by their mannerisms, how they reacted when spoken to by their companions and their general demeanour, all of which would engage her for an hour or more. She liked to think that this self-professed skill greatly aided her when on the shop floor in her beloved emporium.

Pico, not included on the forays to London, remained in Birmingham with Eunice and Dorothy but slightly less spoilt than when his owner was in residence. Marjorie was delighted with the sales figures on her return and vowed to herself to visit London more often; she was well aware that her creation was in solid hands in those of Eunice. This she thought almost every time she returned from a stock buying trip, but had never acted upon it, finding it extremely hard to relinquish control even for a few days, despite knowing that her talented and motivated daughter was at the helm. This aspect of her mother's character did not in the least bother Eunice, as she knew that at some stage in the future, she would be a lady boss.

15

Eunice had many admirers although finding herself not particularly attracted to any of them. The pale, slightly awkward, spaghetti-legged men that she happened upon out and about in Birmingham did not in any way shape or form invite her to engage with them. Preferring a stronger, muscular type with Mediterranean looks, full of bravado and skilful with his hands. The irony of this was not lost on Eunice, as the environs she frequented were certainly not brimming with men of Italian good looks! She was self-assured in all social situations but found herself often bored with a conversation quickly and easily. However, her skilful knack of re-routing a dull exchange was masterly and most often had her smirking to herself when she had completed the conversational manoeuvre.

Swimming at the Moseley Road baths was a pure joy to Eunice. She would try to swim at least once a week, taking the utmost pleasure in metronomically scything through the water, thinking not of low stocks of tan stockings but of simply moving through the water and staying afloat. Marjorie had been insistent that her daughter should learn to swim and be a strong swimmer at that, having been shocked to hear at the age of nine that her cousin Dennis had drowned in the Grand Union Canal.

One morning Eunice had fallen into conversation whilst queuing for a tram with a man in his twenties with a neat moustache and walked as though the pavement was scalding the soles of his boots and missing the middle finger on his left hand which he had ill-advisedly misplaced in a dog's mouth during a pub brawl some years previously. They chatted generally whilst she wondered how he had lost his finger, conjuring up all manner of creative digit-removing scenarios in her head. By the time he got off at his stop at Navigation Road, Eunice was equipped with the knowledge that he was Roland Knapp, twenty-nine and was working for Heads Bookmakers, the unlicensed bookmaker, and an invitation to go racing was on offer, to which she cheerily accepted. Eunice was clear in her head that she was not really attracted to Roland, but he had kept her interest whilst they travelled briefly together on their morning tram journey. One observation she had made, which would have been hard to miss for they were vast, was the size of his hands.

Raceday dawned on a mild and drizzly Saturday in October. And, for her Saturday outing at Bromford Bridge races, Eunice dressed smartly and warmly in her favoured navy Poiret sheen wool coat and taupe cloche hat before setting off to meet Roland at Birmingham New Street station. They would then catch the train to the racecourse.

Eunice had already been to the races a few times with friends, and always enjoyed the theatre and spectacle of the occasion; the sight of the jockeys in their colourful race silks awaiting final riding instructions from the trilby-hatted trainers, the hustle and jostle of the crowds eager to try and win a few quid off the bookmakers, and the pickpocket gangs waiting in the recesses like snipers primed to relieve a racegoer of their possessions.

Being "in the know", Roland was well positioned to put Eunice right in terms of expanding the contents of her purse, which she was eagerly anticipating. Whilst Eunice enjoyed a hot toddy in the Grandstand bar, Roland went off to speak to Finnbar Hickey, a trainer from Cannock Chase, who he had known for many years. Finnbar had been a jockey but was forced into early race retirement by a badly broken leg sustained at Wye racecourse, when the aptly named chestnut mare "Hapless Molly" he was riding, crashed into a wooden post. Subsequently, he now conducted his training business with a pronounced limp. There might have been something wrong with his right leg, but there was little wrong with his brain. He and Roland chatted for some ten minutes or so, the two of them laughing and talking animatedly.

As Roland sat down opposite Eunice in the bar, he smiled and said, 'Right, gal, we are on "Flying Imp" in the 2:30 race, Chris Gordon is riding, and he knows the time of day all right.'

The two of them joined the throng of eager racegoers at the paddock rail and watched the runners parading before the two o'clock race. Eunice fancied a shilling on "The Full Nelson", a striking dark brown horse trained by a Staffordshire trainer, this selection was much against Roland's better judgement. "The Full Nelson" did not trouble the judge and trailed in ninth of the fourteen runners. This left Roland smirking, but he refrained from saying, 'I told you so,' to his race day companion. They just had time to share a pork pie before putting their bets on with Harry Baines, the well-known under-the-counter, Wolverhampton bookmaker.

"Flying Imp" was a big strong, deep-girthed bay gelding, and he had a commanding presence about him as he virtually dragged his stable lad around the paddock, snatching at the lead rein. Eunice, even with her limited equine knowledge, could see he was ready to run a big race. The jockeys filed out of the weighing room into the paddock in readiness to get their final race-riding orders from the trainers and exchange pleasantries with the owners. The owner of "Flying Imp" was a gruff, ruddy-faced man in his sixties and down on the race card as a Mr Patrick Lowndes—he appeared to Eunice as an unpleasant sort of man.

Chris Gordon, a spry and mischievous cheery-looking chap, got a leg up from Finnbar Hickey and settled himself lightly into the saddle. By the time Roland and Eunice had reached the top of the Grandstand, the twelve runners were down at the two-mile start. "Flying Imp" was settled in the third position for the first mile or so and as the runners turned into the straight, Chris gave him a squeeze and his acceleration was effortless, going past the two horses in front of him with disdain, to win by four lengths. The winning connections were clearly very pleased and even Mr Lowndes was looking considerably less gruff. As Chris Gordon left the Winner's Enclosure, he shot Finnbar a brief conspiratory wink and continued jauntily on his way back into the Weighing Room. Eunice and Roland had won a tidy sum and after collecting their winnings they celebrated with Whisky Macs in the King John Inn just outside the racecourse.

On the train journey home, Roland began to laugh and Eunice thought that perhaps he had had one too many whiskies until he said, 'Good job, it didn't rain, gal.'

'Why so? A bit of rain never hurt anyone.'

'Look at the palm of my left hand,' Roland said. As Eunice turned his hand, she could see that it was stained a dark brown colour. She could feel herself becoming irritated as the laughing continued. 'What's going on here then? How do you have this brown staining? Shut up with the laughing.'

'Well, that is what I got after giving "Flying Imp" a well-deserved pat on his way out of the Winners Enclosure.'

Eunice was now antagonised by this annoying conversation and snapped, 'Bloody hell, what on hell's earth are you going on about?'

Roland replied, 'Well, let's just say that Flying Imp was not Flying Imp at all. He was a much faster horse called Henry's Choice who had been given several applications of dark brown dye.' Further loud uproarious laughter continued—this time from the both of them.

Eunice had thoroughly enjoyed her day's racing, relishing the intrigue and shenanigans during the afternoon and eagerly anticipated the thought of the Boxing Day meeting. As Roland attempted to put a reptilian-like arm around her shoulder, this move she had anticipated, she said, 'Roland I have had a terrific day, but I'm not looking for a bedroom buccaneer like you, so it's mates or no deal, okay?'

The arm slowly recoiled, 'All right gal, but I had to try.'

16

James Mumford had found himself a "fancy woman", as the lads at Durent's referred to Rose. Well, she probably was quite fancy in their eyes, none of them being remotely choosy regarding their choice of a female companion after nine pints of Marstons and four pickled eggs on a Saturday night! Rose was Janice's second cousin and had literally bumped into James in Allums the bootmaker, dropping her repaired boots he had bent down to pick up her parcel and then managed to tread on her foot in a state of almost schoolboy excitement. His female interaction was mostly limited to Maude and Ida when they visited him at the farm on a weekend.

As he handed the parcel back to her, he heard the words sort of hiccupping out of the side of his mouth, 'May I buy you a cup of tea to make amends?'

'Well, yes you can and maybe a pair of steel-capped boots too!'

Tea was drunk along with a slice of ginger loaf in Dixons tea room. Whilst this innocent pastime was thoroughly enjoyed by James, he was completely unaware that Rose was in an all-out sting manoeuvre of "setting her cap" at him. She smiled; she laughed at anything remotely amusing that he uttered, flickered her eyelashes as if she were a horse troubled by summer flies and leant across the little wooden table towards him as though she was hard of hearing. Rose could have simply stopped at the smiling, for James was utterly hooked, so captivated was he by this stout apple-shaped and bossy chatterbox of a woman.

Several months later, much to the relief of Maude and to the alarm and annoyance of Kipper Brown, Rose became the second Mrs Mumford, with her chubby frame very much at the heart of proceedings at James's rented small holding. After many years of singledom, Maude was pleased and happy to see her father contented and well-fed. However, Kipper, being Kipper, saw another side to this troubling coupling as not only had he now lost his drinking companion and dog-racing sidekick, but he also saw another aspect to the "pear drop" as he referred to Rose.

She was controlling to the point of absurdity and did her level best to keep Kipper away from her newly acquired husband. James was being pussy-whipped into a stupor of submissiveness and Kipper disliked her intensely, but he was canny enough to bite his tongue and say nothing. He reckoned that his long-standing friend would eventually see the light in the bright realisation of the true nature of this domineering and overbearing woman. So very different was Rose to the comely and still much-missed Margaret.

Of course, Rose had plenty to say on the subject regarding Sylvie, even doing so in front of Maude and Ida when they visited James. Not even this thorny topic escaped Rose's loud brutal opinions and still James appeared content to let her hold court on the subject, not once attempting to rein her in. This induced a lot of awkward fidgeting in Ida and a somewhat feeble attempt by Maude at ignoring Rose, but this was very difficult to do because when she was in full rant it very much resembled a team of runaway plough horses heading her reluctant audience's way. As time went by, both daughter and granddaughter visited less and less leaving Maude and Ida time at the weekends to bake and sew together.

One spring early afternoon, Kipper called by Long Acre in his ramshackle truck to catch up with his old mucker James. Rose was fetching in the washing off the line strung between two plum trees at the back of the cottage. *No sooner was Kipper out of his vehicle, than she was verbally on him, berating the state of the truck, the grubbiness of his clothes, his poor shave and haircut—makes a fella want to go to the pub and never come out*, Kipper thought to himself. He said nothing in response, heading across the yard to the barn to find his friend. The two men headed back to the kitchen, where Rose begrudgingly dispensed weak mugs of tea, whilst wearing a look of displeasure and irritable impatience and making much of folding the wind-fresh laundry.

The conversation stuttered along, peppered with huffing noises from the lady of the house, until she turned from the range and focused her crow-like look on Kipper, informing him that he was going to give her a lift into the village to see Janice without further ado. Kipper, not a religious man, inwardly crossed himself at the same time as praying for a fatal thunderbolt to hit the passenger side of his truck. The short journey began in silence, which suited Kipper well enough indeed hoping that his passenger had been struck mute. It was not until they reached Gibbets Cross that Rose spoke in her habitual passive-aggressive manner, 'I saw her you know.'

'You saw who? What?' Kipper, in no mood for verbal puzzles, snapped back.

'That Sylvie one saw her the evening she went away.'

'Why in hell's teeth have you not said something all these years, are you a deranged woman?' Kipper brought the rattlebox truck to a jarring and abrupt halt on the verge.

'James and his girls are better off without her, a bag of vexation that one. Look how well Ida has turned out without that chancy mare of a mother hindering her.'

Kipper, not a man ever troubled by lack of words, sat shocked and silenced by this stupendous jaw-dropper. Until he said, 'Where on God's earth did you see Sylvie?'

'She was getting on the early evening bus to Birmingham, the one that goes via Wednesbury. It was pretty much dark, but I saw her all right, nobody with her and before you ask, no I'm not telling them, no good it will do my James, Ida, or Maude now. And, if you think about letting them know I will say you made it up. Get this rust box moving, I'm late.' She growled. The last bit of the drive was completed in silence.

Kipper stopped outside of Janice's place and as soon as he had deposited his maddening passenger, he headed immediately to the Blue Boar, the pub not yet open, he went round to the back door and banged on it and eventually Jim, the long-standing landlord, opened it to be greeted by Kipper, 'Get us a whisky Jim will you and make it a large one.'

'You all right, mate?'

'Yes, yes just in need of a restorative.' Kipper took his glass and went and sat by the window whilst Jim went out the back to tend to his racing pigeons. Once the last of the golden liqueur had trickled down the back of Kipper's throat, he began to think about the information he was now in possession of. Thinking pragmatically, he could not see what might be gained after six long years, Sylvie was well gone.

There was the potential satisfaction of exposing Rose as the spiteful keeper of this historic sighting of Sylvie, but she was wise to some less than wholesome transactions that Kipper was party to, and he was well aware that Rose would be in a great hurry to divulge these exploits should he be inclined to corner her. After helping himself to another large whisky from behind the bar, he decided not to reignite the emotional storm of angst and distress and let the proverbial sleeping dogs lie.

James remained blissfully unaware of this troubled and revealing trip into the village, only thinking of the suet meat pudding that would be on his plate later, and the warm demanding body in bed next to him that night.

17

Monday morning, Eunice had the girls enthralled and delighted by her recounting of her day at the races with Roland. Only Lucy had been racing before but all four of them vowed to go before too long. Dina was considerably more interested in how long it was before Roland had had his hand up her dress or at least had tried it on and much laughter ensued.

'He didn't get a look in,' said Eunice laughing and chivvying her team back to work with. 'Come on, girls, we have got new stock to display.'

Marjorie's "Evenings" as she called them (that's when she was not calling them "soirées") had gained great popularity, and she never struggled to fill the sumptuous, upholstered Jacquard club chairs which sat at the card tables in the salon. Although much to a great deal of sniggering from Eunice and the girls, Marjorie had begun to refer to them in a rather grandiose manner as "Gaming Tables".

Martha was becoming quite a mixologist, relishing the work of conjuring up new flavours for the cocktails. Marjorie, however, was mindful to keep a beady eye on her as she was rather keener on the tasting than the serving at times! The party pieces that Divine's mixologist was most proud of were the "Trouser Trampler", a potent concoction of brandy and pear juice and the "Shimmy and Shuffle", a blend of gin, a sugar lump topped off with a vigorous splash of Absinthe.

Marjorie was always meticulous in sticking to her whisky and always keeping her glass close at hand; she had never in her forty-three years been drunk. Forever the control freak, she had a steady hand on all that happened in her sphere and was never one for showing any weakness or vulnerability; in Marjorie's mind, this was for others.

Every morning after waking on the dot of 8:30, she would arrange the pillows in a crest shape against the headboard behind her, lean back and begin a strict self-imposed regime of facial exercises for a full eight minutes, however tired she might be from the previous night's entertaining.

Once out of bed, she applied a generous coating of the compulsory carmine lip colour as she sat at her Venetian Baroque dressing table. Then she set about her pelvic floor exercises but not facing the mirror, even Marjorie was not content to observe herself whilst performing her vaginal callisthenics.

After a loud but reasonably feminine holloa out on the landing, tea appeared delivered by the ever-ready and loyal Dorothy, sometimes she would be dispatched back downstairs to the kitchen, returning with extremely thinly sliced bread, spread with butter and raspberry jam and an equally thinly sliced apple. This most particular breakfast was only consumed if Marjorie was waning in energy or felt that she had a particularly exacting day ahead of her. Dorothy would ready the bath water and after bathing, Marjorie would brush her hair forty-five times with long steady strokes, before arranging it in a Chignon.

Dressing was not a lengthy process as she had thought about this whilst in the bathtub. Her two wardrobes were plentifully stocked with smart, elegant dresses and coats and a separate smaller one housed a multitude of hats and shoes. Wearing stock from Divine she would reiterate regularly that what they sold should be worn with panache and intent. This she did in abundance, although only in her mid-forties, Marjorie had very much the air of a doyenne about her, this she consciously burnished over the years, most satisfactorily.

Once happy with her appearance, she would bid Dorothy goodbye, but not before reminding her of the various tasks that should be tackled in the house that day. Only then could she sally forth to her beloved establishment to keep those profits in a never-ending upward trajectory. If she took a tram to Divine, a wry smile would appear on her immaculately made-up face as she recalled receiving the news of George's untimely but most convenient tram accident. In her youthful wildest daydreams, she could not have hoped for a speedier nor more opportune outcome on targeting George in that long cinema queue.

Most days she would take Pico with her to work, but if it was a day when a card evening was planned, then she would leave him with Dorothy. This was because Pico had a most unfortunate tendency to occasionally cock his leg on the smart-suited legs of Marjorie's male guests thereby rendering the salon to give out the rather unpleasant and pungent smell of a men's urinal; the very opposite of what Marjorie was trying to create!

As time-consuming as it was, and it always had to be carried out after the shop closed at 4:30 in the afternoon, Eunice and her mother liked to change the window display on a monthly basis "to keep it tasty" as Peggy would laughingly say.

Eunice thoroughly enjoyed this task as it enabled her creative flair to flourish, but it could so often be somewhat stifled by Marjorie's overbearing and controlling manner given her less-than-creative approach. The two of them coming to blows over the smallest of details such as the colour of the stockings worn by the mannequins or the shoes and gloves. It was usually by a fine feat of persuasiveness that Eunice got the final decision, reminding her mother that sales had rocketed that month, new customers having been lured into Divine by her, Eunice's original and charming dinner party setting for the evening wear, which had been achieved whilst Marjorie was dealing with the latest crisis in Donald's utterly complicated lifestyle.

Each month there was a different theme or season, which obviously included the Christmas festivities and an Easter scenario. If the windows required a complex set, then Lucy's cousin Thomas, a joiner, could turn his hand to just about anything, and as it happened lay his other hand on just about anything which included all sorts of props, sleighs, chandeliers, stuffed foxes, rabbits, and birds. During the month of May, Eunice would create a luscious, colourful garden party scene with dried and fresh flowers and plants. The mannequins were in an elegant sitting pose about to drink tea from beautiful bone China teacups, all brought into the store by Dorothy from Marjorie's dining room sideboard. All this was to entice new and old customers to be lured into purchasing a fabulous outfit in which to sparkle, perhaps even for a trip to the Chelsea Flower Show.

July brought about a summer wedding scene. Marjorie would have the bride in a modest gown, which Elsie had mocked up, so as not to draw attention to the bride but to all of Divine's finest chiffon and silk dresses, and chic Parisian hats. As for Marjorie, it was all about focusing on the wedding guests and their outfits.

These two large glass bow shop windows, on either side of the door, also invariably featured men in the displays. Divine made a special point of welcoming men, as it was them, in particular, who most often bankrolled these expensive purchases which left the shop in pale lilac boxes, tissue paper and bags adorned with cream ribbon.

18

Ida continued to blossom, now eleven she was very much her own person. A good-looking girl sporting her mother's luxuriant brown hair and the green eyes of a cat. The school day was enjoyed rather than endured, sharp and engaging; she was as adept at manipulating Mrs Sampson, her class teacher, as she was at getting the boys to give her their last few hard-won toffees.

Her closest school friend was Wilma Dowson whose family ran the hardware shop. Wilma, smaller and less confident than Ida, was in awe of her friend and certainly not brave, or bold enough, to go on the surreptitious swimming trips to Teversham's lake, however much Ida pleaded with her to go with them.

Frank and Molly, Wilma's parents, liked their daughter's best friend well enough but Molly was alert to Ida's obvious wayward tendencies and did her level best to hinder the burgeoning friendship. If Ida had tea after school at the Dowson's, she was always polite and well mannered, Maude and Elmer had seen to that forever saying, 'Manners maketh man and woman too.'

Of course, Ida was, at least locally, burdened by the legacy of her mother's fast and loose reputation. All eyes peeled to see if they could be the first to say, 'Ah, there she goes, that girl is most definitely cut from the same cloth as her errant mother.'

Speculation on the once hot subject of the identity of Ida's father had ceased long ago, to the relief of Elmer and Maude. This particular bonfire was only poked by the odious Rose from time to time.

Despite Elmer's lack of worldliness and considering he spent the largest part of his working day with a horse's leg between his knees, he had been alerted to Rose's masterly exploitation skills of James from his very first meeting with her. Fortunately, their paths rarely crossed, Rose busy in the full-time occupation of keeping James's nose to the grindstone and just where she wanted him, under the full force of her thumb!

Maude's personality rendered her happiest sitting on the proverbial fence when it came to commenting on her stepmother's more scheming attributes. The reality was that with the disagreeable Rose now bustling about James's kitchen, she was now much less, or at least felt less, responsible for her father's well-being.

Kipper, having just dropped off some fencing posts at Durent's, was feeling particularly pleased with his day's dealings, having "acquired" the fencing at an extraordinarily good price ensuring a very tidy mark-up to him. He was running through in his head as to which pub he would frequent that evening when they opened when he spotted the "Pear Drop" leaving the grocers.

Stopping the truck, he got out and said to Rose curtly, 'We need a word, get in,' opening the passenger door.

'You can drive me home then we might have a word if I'm so inclined,' she said as she heaved herself up into the dirty cab and sat down heavily.

Kipper drove about a mile and a half before stopping the truck in a gateway. He turned to Rose and said, 'What you told me back along, you told anyone else? What about Janice told her?'

Rose, sneeringly, said, 'If we are talking about the same thing, that hussy, then the answer is no! Told nobody but you.'

'What were you doing telling me for?' Kipper replied.

There was a pause until she said, with a snigger in her voice, 'Aha, I just felt like it.'

Kipper was angry, 'Get out of my truck. I am not driving you any further.' With that, he got out, taking the keys out of the ignition and promptly walked back in the direction of the village to await the opening of the pubs. Thinking as he walked, would James ever see what others saw? Should he go and talk to Janice? By the time he reached the village pond, he had decided once more that he would do nothing and say nothing.

19

Janice did not particularly enjoy her work at Roy Barclays, but Roy had a soft spot for her, and her day was not onerous, and in turn, she was sweet on Charlie, the Barclay's only offspring. Not that he would notice this gathering steam of affection, as he was far too engrossed in his passion for catching anything he could with a rod and line.

Many surreptitiously acquired steaks had seen their way into the stomach of Owen Butters and his family without cost, thus ensuring a plentiful amount of fishing on the Teversham Estate. Charlie would spend hours in the back room of his parent's house, researching the joyful art of making and tying fishing flies, creating beautiful pheasant tail flies, and carefully creating bronze mallard feather flies to outwit trout. Hours of his spare time would be spent meandering in the countryside with his head down, his eyes peeled for interesting bird plumage utterly oblivious to the burning yearning of his father's employee.

Janice had been good friends with Sylvie throughout their school years, but she was not entirely sure that she could say that she absolutely knew her. For sure, they had larked about together and giggled about boys during the village cricket matches, when Janice was roped into help with the cricket teas, her father being Captain of the team. But there was something about her friend that Janice could just not define, sometimes aloof and at other times full-scale engagement and enthusiasm.

Sylvie had spent the day with Janice and her family helping with the cider apple harvest, somewhat reluctantly on Sylvie's part. Whilst Janice's mother Bernice was observing Sylvie juggling glossy Dabinet cider apples that she was supposed to be putting in the collecting baskets, Janice overheard her saying, 'She is a minx if ever I saw one.'

As Roy's ardour for Janice grew, so did her passion for Charlie gather pace. This tricky triangle of ardent fervour was nothing but a pot at boiling point. This pot finally came to a boil on a hot August day, always a difficult day in a butcher shop with heat, flies, and customers only interested in buying cold ham.

Janice was serving a young boy Harold, who had been dispatched by his mother to buy six slices of the predictable ham. As she was taking the thin slices off the slicer and onto the brown paper, she dropped a piece, as she bent over to retrieve it, little did she know that this was the very same moment that Roy Barclay was intently watching her attractive peach-like backside almost boring a hole through her apron and underwear. Meanwhile, Mrs Barclay was watching her husband in his intense reverie. Roy Barclay had been under the misapprehension that his wife was at home doing the monthly accounts.

'Roy Barclay, what in damnation are you playing at? Get out the back this very second,' she bellowed at him.

What followed was a verbal battering of some considerable force, as this berating reached its pinnacle, Mrs

Barclay was the colour of an overripe raspberry, whilst her husband attempted a stuttering defence. In truth, he had no defence, guilty as charged, but he gave a vaguely plausible excuse in that he thought he could see a cracked tile over by the mincer; in truth, the mincer was nowhere near Janice's backside!

The sorry outcome of this perving saga was that a dull, young apprentice devoid of initiative was taken on and Janice was "let go" with two months' pay and a brusque "good luck" from Mrs Barclay and a wink from her husband.

Janice took this in her stride; she knew all she needed to know about cuts of meat and men by now. All this yelling and drama amongst her employers brought about a dawning realisation in her, that she was wasting her time on the fishing-obsessed Charlie, who at the time of Roy Barclay's lustful gazing episode was trying his luck on the river Brean with his latest fly creation.

20

Roland naively believed that perseverance almost always paid off when it came to the opposite sex. To be fair, it had been done on occasions, but he had never encountered a girl quite like Eunice before. He would be waiting outside Divine when Eunice was locking up the store. Whilst he potentially might have been a fun nocturnal diversion, Eunice felt his skills lay not in the bedroom, but in his unscrupulous and artful mind. She was sure that she may well have need of his duplicity at some point in the future.

So it became a duel of sorts with Eunice never giving so much as a "full inch" but subtly instilling in him that he was after all making some small progress with her. This situation was helped by the fact that Roland was under the heavy misapprehension that he was irresistible to women of all ages. He had cultivated a pencil moustache which he was forever admiring each time he walked past a shop window; that was when he wasn't reading the Sporting Life paper. Unbeknownst to him, Eunice loathed moustaches, calling them thigh grazers!

Lucy, Dina, Peggy, and Martha enjoyed this sea-saw charade most especially when Roland, sensing that he was losing ground, would give Eunice the "heads up" on a winning horse. This privileged information was eagerly and promptly passed onto the quartet, and in their staggered lunch breaks they would place their bets with Tony Leatham, the bookmaker who "ran a book" in the Bull and Dragon pub on the corner of Slade Road. This supplemented their income handsomely.

All four of the girls flirted openly and outrageously with Roland, much to the amusement of Eunice. Meanwhile, Marjorie was totally unaware of the ongoing games, as she spent her time concentrating on planning the next card evening and the continued uplift in Divine's fortunes.

Eunice had mentioned Roland in passing to her mother commenting, 'Roland the bookie's runner fella might be useful.'

'Good girl, keep him handy without him getting handy!' Marjorie had said with a laugh.

The girls were careful not to place bets with Roland's boss, the fierce Edgar Bennett, so sharp he hardly needed a razor blade in the mornings! Should Edgar get a whiff of what Roland was up to, he would be long gone and so would the healthy additions to the girls' wages. Men like Roland were dispensable, ten a penny lurking on almost every street corner, and Eunice and Marjorie knew this, and Roland did not.

21

Marjorie Peyton was not her birth name, Maggie Hollit as she was known when she met George in the cinema queue, had changed her name after she left Walsall. She felt that "Maggie Hollit" was not going to take her as far as Marjorie wanted to go!

Her father had left her mother when she was eleven, following years of domestic beer-fuelled bodily harm and general brutish behaviour. The labouring jobs he took never lasted very long before the foreman let him go yet again. Marjorie's mother did the best she could working long hours in a laundry but leaving her daughter to fend for herself resulted in Marjorie becoming very streetwise and developing the ability to judge a person's character quickly and astutely. As a girl, she was always streets ahead of her peers in outlook and appearance. Men generally garnered little respect from Marjorie; she vowed to herself that she would never be treated poorly by a man.

Her class teacher, Mrs McConnell, had identified Marjorie as a pupil who had the drive and determination to exceed in whatever she set out to do with her life. The humdrum routine of a domestically talented wife was never on Marjorie's radar. However, she was single-minded and socially aware enough to realise that a marriage of convenience and opportunity would be of necessity to get to where she wanted to go—but just once!

The upstairs salon at Divine, as Marjorie called it, was very much her domain. Warmed in the winter months by a coal fire, it was a comfortable and elegant room almost baroque in style. There was always a vase of lilies on the centre table, her favourite, casting a heady scent around the room. A drinks cabinet sat to the left of her desk, heavy with crystal tumblers, port glasses and a set of six Highball glasses, together with bottles of whisky, gin, port and other favoured tipples.

From time to time, Marjorie did venture downstairs to the showroom; she rarely referred to it as the shop, preferring the elevated status of "showroom". Her trips downstairs were reserved for her biggest spending customers which, of course, came as no surprise to her team. A handful of women who considered themselves friends would frequent the shop, but none of these women could ever really say that they knew Marjorie particularly well. One of them often called her the Pangolin, in reference to their protective scales, nocturnal lifestyle and large tongue. Marjorie needed very little sleep and was a splendid talker particularly when there was a sale on the horizon!

Other than her brief forays downstairs, Marjorie kept meticulous order books and accounts and spent several hours a day reading the provincial Midlands and National newspapers. She believed that the art of a thorough general knowledge conversation with clients was an essential and very useful tool. So she also encouraged the girls to read these papers whilst they ate their lunch in the kitchen rather than "gaggling" as Marjorie called gossiping. Which, of course, they loved to do, but never in Marjorie's earshot.

On the kitchen table, in the middle of the linen cloth, there was always, so long as Eunice could source them, a large glass bowl of fresh lemons. This detail Marjorie was a stickler for.

The girls were allowed to smoke, but not downstairs and never in the street. Barney, the milkman, delivered milk and a quart of cream each day except on Sundays. Eunice adored cream in her coffee, imagining a Parisian café crème as she drank it. The lunch break was half an hour which the girls had arranged into a staggered rota, an hour was allowed if they were working late, or helping at one of Marjorie's Wednesday or Thursday evening soirées.

Eunice had nothing but admiration and the most utter respect for her mother. She saw the long hours that Marjorie had worked when she was a child and had treasured their Sunday outings together. Marjorie was a lifelong atheist, so Sunday church was never an option. Her mother had always prayed out loud when she was being knocked around and little good it had done her.

Eunice had her mother's work ethic and determination to succeed but was certainly more light-hearted. She spoke quickly in a low monotone Birmingham accent, of which she was always conscious, whereas Marjorie had tried to cultivate a more universal clipped accent which she had tutored herself to master during her early teenage years which were spent hanging around the smartest environs of the city.

Once she was her mother's right- and left-hand woman, Eunice had helped to find some of the girls who worked at Divine. The prospective sales assistants had two interviews, the first of which was with Marjorie upstairs in the salon. This was a deliberate ploy by her to see if the girls were in any way unnerved by the elaborate surroundings. If they were nervous shrinking violets or brash, they would certainly not make the second interview with Eunice down in the showroom. The girls were rarely reserved or timorous as Eunice would not have engaged them for an initial interrogation by her mother if they had been.

Peggy had got talking to Eunice in the bakery on Bell Street, mentioning that she was looking to leave her tedious job at Dempsey's Ironmongery, which Eunice could have successfully bet she disliked intensely. She was an instant hit with both the Peyton ladies with her unique personality which was confident yet with an underlay of vulnerability. Peggy was loose-limbed with a wonderfully long neck and almost olive skin. This Marjorie felt would be an excellent trait when dealing with customers particularly the men who popped in to collect or buy a gorgeous dress for their long-suffering wives.

Dina would understudy Eunice if she had a day off sick, which was a rare occurrence given her sterling drive and work ethic. Dina had the most splendid thick strawberry blonde hair, inherited from her Irish father. She exuded a quiet command of the task at hand when she was helping a customer with a choice of dresses, with the client relaxing knowing that they were in a safe pair of hands. They always left happy and delighted at their Divine experience.

Lucy, originally from Derby, had just called in one afternoon at the shop. She had an edge to her along with a razor-sharp wit, and her long legs were the envy of the other girls. During Lucy's interview, Eunice had felt that the girl's candid way and steeliness would ensure she excelled even with the trickier customers. Eunice's instinct was correct, with Lucy cheerily serving the more demanding ladies with ease and a viper-like tendency to get the sale closed.

Martha, with her rhythmic Scottish accent, always saw the humour in any situation, but she had the intelligence to know when not to use it. She had a large bosom and good strong legs, the sort of legs that would take her up the steepest of Munros without turning a hair—not that she was inclined to any sort of exercise other than vigorously using the cocktail shaker in the salon at one of Marjorie's Wednesday evening gatherings.

Occasionally Marjorie would arrange an evening of cards, at which she was unsurprisingly competitive, although wily enough to keep this urge to win in check so as not to dissuade the other players from attending. If a cash poker game was scheduled, she upped her play considerably and a masterclass in "game face" played out all whilst sipping a large malt whisky. Occasionally leaving the card table in the salon to top up her carmine red lipstick, which she always wore, prompting Martha to quip to Lucy, 'I reckon Mrs P sleeps with her lipstick on.'

As Marjorie became increasingly successful, she developed a slight haughtiness. Eunice became aware of this about a year after she began to work with her mother. This singularity was never in evidence at home, Marjorie being much more relaxed and unwound when not at her emporium, but always in place was the carmine red lipstick.

22

James Mumford was beginning, ever so slowly, to see his life just a little bit from Kipper's point of view. The trips to the greyhound track and pubs, so sternly curtailed by Rose, were initially a trade-off for the delights on the kitchen table and her voracious sexual appetite.

If truth be told, James had fared pretty well as a widower living on his own as he had. Never without a friend or fellow "horse coper" calling in to pass the time of day and always finding a mate to sup a Saturday night pint with. What with a good few kind-spirited women of Marshcombe baking for him, not to mention Maude's legendary pies and cakes, James reckoned life had been pretty good. Then Rose came along.

After about three years, the domestic tyranny of his second wife began to buff the gloss off the benefits exchange, so he decided one morning, as he was milking Dolly the Jersey house cow, that he would endeavour "to get his balls back" as Kipper might have said. And he would do his best to be a reluctant participant in Rose's long-winded rapacious and hoggish sex acts.

James did not impart any of this to Kipper as he knew what the response was likely to be: 'Ha ha…well, let us see matey how well that goes. Good luck!'

Of course, as each month passed James's resolve ebbed and flowed, if cider had been drunk his willpower to "regain" his testicles diminished considerably. He did successfully, however, begin to spend less and less time at the kitchen table, he would almost inhale his meals and be back outside just about before his last sip of tea had hit his oesophagus!

This change in his demeanour was not unnoticed by Rose, who initially upped her stove creations by adding luscious amounts of butter and cream to meals and increasing her husband's helping. Regularly produced her very delicious rabbit stew or her infamous "two-way dumpling", consisting of damson jam at one end and bacon at the other. It seems that subconsciously she thought that if she could feed him like a "Foie Gras Goose" filling him with a stomach full of grub, he would be so stupefied, that he would be unable to harness the wherewithal to get back out to the yard and animals, and unable to move away when she might jump on him. But the plan somehow failed to achieve the results Rose wished for as James, however full and bloated he might have felt, always managed to don his leather field coat, lace his boots, and return to his treasured horses.

With so much sullen huffiness from an irritated and frustrated wife, James had become fully aware that a fine rope would have to be walked where Rose's feelings and actions were concerned, sensing in his clumsy and unworldly way, that Rose was not a woman to make an enemy of—most especially if you were married to her!

23

Marjorie, although an exacting and demanding taskmistress, had a hidden and more nurturing element to her. Actively encouraging Lucy, Dina, Peggy, Martha and, of course, Eunice to better themselves. Not that she felt swimming was going to help her daughter much. She was keen that they should broaden their skills and gain knowledge. All the girls had attended school until the age of fourteen, but in Peggy and Martha's case somewhat sporadically. Dina, when in school sat in a stupefied reverie staring out of the window at the coal merchant's opposite.

Lucy had loved singing from a young age, and as an eight-year-old, she had first experienced the sheer joy of singing in the Steepleton Orphanage school choir. If there was a tune being hammered out on the ivories in the pub however crudely, Lucy would be up from the bench and her friends, and straight into a delightful serenade despite the pianist's limited musical skills.

Keen to enhance the enjoyment of her soirées, Marjorie was happy for Lucy to come in a bit later one Tuesday morning a month so that she could take a lesson with singing coach Josephine Hoffmeir. These lessons she loved, with Peggy quipping, 'Oh she will be top of the bill at the Theatre Royal in no time. I hope she wangles us lot free seats!'

24

Janice, freed from the lecherous behaviour of Roy Barclay, and the hapless lack of interest from Charlie, had taken herself off to Birmingham. Lodging initially with Freda Sterry, an old friend of her mother's, she quickly found work at the Midlands Vinegar factory, armed as she was with a veritable glowing shiny reference from the "happy to see Janice on her way" Mrs Barclay, she cake-walked the interview. So began the next five years of her life, smelling of vinegar.

There was a lingering hope that the move to the veritable metropolis of Birmingham might somehow magically conjure up coming across Sylvie. In her mind, it was the most obvious place for her to head to. Janice still inwardly winced when she recalled the typically harsh names the racing lads had called Sylvie behind her back and more frequently in the initial few weeks after her leaving Ida on her own. "Raleigh" was the one they bantered about most often, (the bike company, Raleigh's tagline was "for speed and ease"). She could not walk past one of those bikes without thinking of her old friend's zeal for life.

All Janice could hope for was that the men of the City of Birmingham found the smell of soured wine attractive!

25

Donald would always recall the day he met Marjorie. He was adjusting the flower display of stunning spring blooms outside his shop when she appeared to sashay towards him with a determined and fixed gaze in his direction.

'Mr Puckett people tell me you are known as "Mr Bloom", so I felt that I should come and see what you are all about,' said Marjorie as she extended a bedazzled hand, in a rather thrustingly way, towards Donald and giving him a man-sized handshake.

He was somewhat side-swiped by this overtly confident and somewhat mesmerising woman. 'Please, do come into the shop, I am Donald, you can call me Donald, have never like my surname, now how may I help you today?'

'Well, now Donald, why don't you show me what you have,' which she could see perfectly well, standing as she was in front of two dozen copper flower containers brimming with an abundance of colourful cut flowers.

'I will be requiring fresh flowers regularly for Divine Gowns, my shop on Forde Street, perhaps you know it?'

Donald replied in a very friendly manner, 'Indeed, I do. Such wonderful and very tempting window displays I always think when passing by.'

Unbeknown to Donald, he could not have paid the Chatelaine of Divine a better or bigger compliment.

After selling her a dozen yellow roses and a very large bunch of lilies that day, they had become unlikely close friends. Two people you would be hard to find more different, Donald small framed, with thin sandy hair, rather shy and quietly spoken, drawn as he was to Marjorie's force of nature and at times strident approach.

He secretly admired her fortitude and fierce business mind; his neat little shop on Miller Road did all right; and he was proud of Bright Blooms bringing a little cheer into people's homes.

Donald lived in the house on Doidge Road that he had been born in, a solitary only child, something of a delicate mother's boy. Choosing to continue living there after both his parents died from lung cancer. His friendship with Marjorie and Eunice brought a little frisson into his otherwise rather quiet life.

It was some six months after they had met, when Donald confided in Eunice that he would absolutely love to buy a dress, hat, and gloves to wear at home. Eunice, not broadsided in the slightest, said she would speak to her mother about his unusual but interesting purchasing request. She knew exactly what Marjorie's response would be, 'Look my girl, you know as well as I do—a sale is a sale so pop into Bright Blooms on your way home and tell him we would be delighted to welcome him to Divine on Thursday after closing.'

It was not long before a not-inconsiderable sum of Donald's life savings had been spent in the opulent surroundings of Divine Gowns, so much, so he that had to buy a second wardrobe from Headleys Furniture shop. He looked after these clothes as though they were royal heirlooms, wearing them with joy and a thrilling excitement whilst doing his household chores.

26

Janice adapted swiftly and remarkably easily to busy city life, thriving on the hustle and rattle of the noisy Birmingham streets. Her working day began at eight as she joined the sometimes-cheery band of girls heading into the Midlands Vinegar factory. The work in the bottling plant was mind-numbingly repetitive and dull but the girls working on her "line" were full of back chat and lively banter amongst the clatter of bottles.

She was relieved and pleased to learn from Vera, who worked alongside her, that Mr Rollick, the bottling foreman, was nothing like Roy Barclay; keeping all his body parts very much to himself, quiet and respectful in his directions. Of course, Vera and the others loved to say at least once a day, 'Will it be today that one of us gets a bollicking off Mr Rollick?'

Janice walked part of the way to work, loving the chance to people watch, before hopping on a tram at Sixways which delivered her to the imposing wrought iron factory gates. She worried daily that the vinegary perfume that clung to her would be a repellent, but she found out one nippy February evening on her return tram journey to Sixways that vinegar was very clearly an alluring pheromone to some of the male population of the city. As she stood ready to hop off at her stop, she felt a steady warm pressure through her dress and mauve winter coat, at the point of her coccyx. Swinging round with the speed of a seasoned professional ballerina she saw a short middle-aged man with a moustache, his face gurning and sweaty despite the evening chill.

As quickly as she had swung round, she swung back again, and in a deft Latin dance manoeuvre jumped backwards and with all the force she could muster rammed the heel of her shoe into the top of his foot, then ground it down as if putting out a reluctant lit cigarette butt. Without turning round again Janice reached her stop and stepped off the tram. Laughing as she walked on, thinking who knew that working in Roy Barclay's butcher shop would give her such varied and resourceful life skills. This would be a good story to tell Vera and the rest of them in their tea break.

27

Occasionally, one of Divine's customers might bring their reluctant but helpfully wealthy husbands with them, or as in the case of Phyllida Speilman, her extremely helpfully wealthy "fancy man". When this occurred, Eunice would ignite her "entertain the gent" formulae. Most often a discreet raising of her right eyebrow in the direction of Martha who would get the ball rolling. Martha was a demon chess, draughts, and domino player. A small table and two gilt chairs would appear, and the husband would be offered the game of his choosing.

In laying this on, there was the potential risk of disgruntling the wife, as Martha sat chatting engagingly, but this never occurred and very often an extra gown was added to the list of purchases, particularly if the gentleman had imbibed plenty of the proffered alcohol from the salon.

Martha had grown up in a pub, mingling with the customers collecting drained pint mugs and playing dominoes and sometimes draughts with the male drinkers. She knew almost instantly how to temper her game, letting the gentleman win of course, but not without a bit of a battle on the board and an inward smile to herself. During the course of Martha's game with the men, it was the ideal opportunity to let them know ever so discreetly about the mid-week evening card soirées held upstairs.

Phyllida Speilman had once had glittering reveries about becoming the next Kate Carney. Her main obstacle in this fantasy is that her enthusiasm for entertainment was not matched by any fragment of talent. So, after many humiliating dismal auditions, she lowered her lofty ambitions settling for being the best-dressed failed music hall star in the Midlands, a role she mastered to a high standard. Phyllida managed extremely skilfully to conduct a regular quartet of admirers. None of these four amours knowing of the other. The girls and Marjorie all greet the "man of the moment", squiring Phyllida through the splendid double doors of Divine, with welcoming beaming smiles.

28

Ida and Maude had a very special bond between them, made all the stronger by Maude's natural maternal instinct. Elmer and Maude had passed the point of hope, in regard to the two of them ever creating a baby between them.

Fellow Wednesday Marshcombe market shoppers, with their heads tilted to one side as if in patronising empathy, whilst they wrangled their dribbling nosed broods by their coat collars to the hardware stall, had stopped passing comments such as, 'No Little Elmers yet then, Maude?'

Deep down Maude wished that Ida might be rather more needy than she was. Never really seeming to desire a great deal of reassurance or affirmation. The bond was held more strongly by Maude, who was more than aware that Ida just felt an obligation of affection to her aunt and uncle. She was so like Sylvie in so many respects that the inner core of self-reliance and containment was very evident to Maude, and it was not lost on her that these characteristics would serve Ida well in life. She consoled herself with the thought that perhaps her and Elmer's consistent care and quasi-parental guidance had at least instilled a semblance of normality in Ida's life.

Ida genuinely did not think of her mother. She was curious and inquiring by nature, but on the subject of her parents, she had no interest. She never mentioned her mother, seemingly perfectly happy to render Sylvie to the very furthest recess of her brain. If her granda mentioned Sylvie in front of her, she would act as though he was talking about a stranger to her. Once in the schoolyard during playtime, Jonny Willet, a tall boy, thin as a leek said, 'Ida, where's your ma and da?'

'Jonny Willet, I don't know, and I don't care. Aunt Maude and Uncle Elmer look after me now. Giv'us one of your apples, Jonny.' Dropping her skipping rope, she snatched an apple out of his lunch box.

Swimming, in the summer months, became one of Ida's favourite pastimes, growing stronger and as fit as any of the boys, often beating her peers in races across Teversham's lake. James taught her to ride, but although a natural fit on a horse, she did not really enjoy it. This was not helped by Rose's unnecessary and loud verbal critique as she leant on the paddock gate whilst James gave the riding lesson. Not that Rose had ever sat on a horse herself!

The most rhythmic repetitive motion of the sewing machine very often brought Maude to a sort of trance-like state, only broken by either Mrs Noble coming to issue an instruction or by reoccurring worries of what had happened to her sister. Elmer had always been reluctant to speculate and would most often just close the conversation down if Maude tried to discuss her sister's fate further with her husband. She felt as though Elmer, as reasonable a man as he was, was about to bang the kitchen table with his fists every time the subject came up. He was undeniably content to believe that Ida was his and Maude's child.

Kipper began to do two things, to look out for Ida, not realising that this act of kindness was unnecessary as she was exemplary at looking out for herself. And the other was to avoid Rose, which was a trickier task to do if he wanted to speak to James, who had in the past provided Kipper with discreet storage for some of his less than honestly acquired goods! This arrangement was now relocated to an old lime pit situated on the boundary of James's land in the far corner of Welham Field, which Kipper could reach from the green lane undetected by prying eyes and pear-shaped wives!

Kipper had never fancied a wife of his own, honestly acquired or not! This long-held belief only held more firmly after witnessing James' descent into part emasculation. He was not a bad sort of looking man, not overly tall, rather stocky, and solid in fact. The type of man who filled a pub doorway with his presence. Fair skinned, his large hands speckled with a thousand freckles and the smoker's fingers of his right hand turned a dirty hessian colour. He was content to rent a box of a place from the Cartwrights, out at their mill in Bearstone.

Kipper's reputation for alleviating the boredom of some of the more adventurous-minded housewives of Marshcombe, was not unwarranted. More often than not, he left quietly by their back door, with a ginger cake, a large pork pie and a jar of homemade tomato chutney under one arm whilst the smiling provider of these home-baked goods waved goodbye equally quietly. Thus, keeping himself happily sustained in more ways than one for days at a time!

29

Roland had never attempted to hide the fact that he had been on the receiving end of an illuminating and somewhat educational' stay in Winston Green Prison. This "holiday" was endured when he was twenty-three. The vast and gloom-filled prison was something of an eye-opener even to Roland, serving an eight-month sentence, with a year suspended, for impersonating a jewellery dealer alongside fraud and deception for good measure. A master from a young age of striking up a conversation with anybody, he had engineered a chat with a "well-to-do" looking elderly lady in Taylor's Tea House one Saturday afternoon, called Daphne Selkis.

He had commented on how lovely her ruby and pearl ring looked, and before she could finish thanking him for the compliment, Roland was asking the pretty young waitress to bring another cup and saucer to Daphne's tea table. He felt that fortune was beaming down upon him, as he straightened his tie and pulled the chair up under him, thinking as he did so to keep his elbows off the table and not leave the teaspoon in his cup. *This lady looks well posh in her glossy mink stole and elaborately embroidered coat,* he thought.

The two unlikely acquaintances chatted about this and that, with Roland endeavouring to not make hideous slurping noises, something that his sister had pulled him up on many times before.

'Have you lived in Birmingham long?' he ventured.

'I am originally from Sevenoaks in Kent, but I met my late husband, Wilfred Selkis at Paddington Station. When we married, I left Kent behind. Birmingham has been my home for forty-three years now.'

Good, thought Roland to himself, *Daphne likes to natter, and she is widowed, just how I like 'em!*

Responding to one of Daphne's many questions that she put to her young tea-drinking companion, he heard himself saying, 'Brummie through and through me. No, not found myself a good wife yet, but I'm looking hard. Have always worked in the gem business, have a small workshop over Bignall Road way.'

'Ah, I see now why my ring caught your highly trained eye. My departed Wilfred gifted me many lovely pieces over the years, and this ring is one of my favourites. You know, this is such a coincidence, Trevor, as I had been thinking about getting my jewellery appraised and valued. Is that something that you might be able to assist me with?'

'Well, Mrs Selkis, that most certainly is.'

They arranged for Roland to visit Daphne the following week at her home in Edgbaston. Roland was anxious to leave Taylors on his own, he could not run the risk of coming across someone who knew him and then saying, 'Hello, Roland mate, how are things with you?' as that afternoon he was grifting as his alias Trevor.

The following Tuesday morning promptly and smartly dressed; Roland knocked on the immaculate black front door of Daphne Selkis's Regency style townhouse. The door was swiftly opened, it did briefly cross Roland's mind that Daphne had been waiting immediately behind it. 'Good morning, Trevor, thank you for coming; do come in.'

They sat down at the highly polished oak table in the dining room. Where laid out on a lace doily was a readied pot of coffee, milk, sugar, and cups, alongside several pieces of jewellery. Roland hated coffee but accepted a cup along with three teaspoons of sugar to disguise the taste.

Glimmering slightly in the weak mid-morning sun, were two pearl strings, one short and one long, placed amongst other pieces. Roland had made the foresightful decision to buy a jeweller's eyeglass and a thin-papered cheap receipt book. These he made much of as he set them down on the table in a semi-business-like manner. Picking up a French silver "Pense à Moi" he examined it declaring it, 'Very handsome, Mrs Selkis.'

'That was a wedding gift. What do you think of this ring, Trevor?' Daphne chirped, handing him a beautiful garnet ring.

'Very fine, very fine indeed.' Roland now felt very much out of his depth and could feel several globules of sweat forming on his forehead despite it being October. He then brought a striking opal and gold, pink tourmaline ring towards his face and examined it with the eyeglass and followed this with a platinum filigree broach.

'Well, what do you think, Trevor?'

Roland, who was fighting an overwhelming urge to bolt into the hallway for the front door, said as slowly as he could muster, 'Well, Mrs Selkis, as you said yourself, they are fine pieces. I would like to take them back to my workshop and do a full valuation for you.' Snatching his receipt book he asked for a pen, somewhat idiotically without waiting for her response.

'Trevor, if you think that is the best way to proceed then let's do that.' she said enthusiastically.

'Do you have a pen; I seem to have mislaid mine.' Roland never having owned an ink pen in his life was more of a pencil man. He then asked Daphne if she would write the receipt out as he had sprained his writing wrist chopping firewood! This she did, making sure that the carbon copy paper was in place. On handing the book back to Roland, he tore off the top copy and gave it ceremoniously to Daphne. He folded the jewellery up in the doily and put it into a small black drawstring bag saying as he did so, 'Left my briefcase in the workshop.'

After shaking her by the hand, Roland was down the pavement like a hunted gazelle leaving No. 4 Beech Crescent far behind him.

However, unbeknownst to Roland but definitely most fortunate for Daphne, when he had taken the receipt book out of his pocket, he had dropped his post office savings book in his real name—Roland Knapp. This turn of events led to a policeman knocking on Roland's backyard door and a trip to Duddeston Police Station. Also, fortunately for Daphne, due to her swift reaction to finding the savings book, Roland had not had time to visit Jack Knox, a very accommodating "jewellery fence".

On leaving Winston Green Prison, Roland was far better educated than when he had arrived.

30

When Ida wasn't at school helping out at Mrs Noble's or hurtling about the lanes on an old bicycle James had given her, she spent time sketching dresses. The village school did not do art lessons, the children occasionally being told to draw copies of fauna and flora that were laid out on a table at the back of the classroom. Maude encouraged this pastime, hoping that Ida might have a true talent for drawing as she called it. Observing that the rural enchantments would not hold her sister's daughter for long, once she had left school.

Ida would bamboozle her way into the Dowsons', much to the exasperation of Mrs Dowson and get the beguiled Wilma to pose for her, draped in lengths of material loaned by Mrs Noble, who secretly had much admiration and time for Ida. She did all she could to help and encourage the lively, cheerful girl who had done much of her growing up in the Noble workshop.

Grace Noble had a grown-up son, Sam, who worked as a slaughter man in Nuneaton, but she and her husband Fred, saw almost nothing of him as their daughter-in-law Enda was frail as a Crane Fly. When Sam wasn't working, he was taking care of his wife and smelling of carcasses. Grace hoped with all her heart that Ida would make something of herself. Daily she was reminded of what a good selfless soul Maude was.

Ida found a great deal of thrill in getting her own way, without the other person realising this. Wilma hardly fell into this category as she did not represent the least bit of a challenge. So, in awe was Wilma of her sporting, confident school friend. The bigger high for Ida, was when she successfully coerced an adult, the greater the challenge of the person's personality the better. This manipulation of elders and peers was not always necessarily to her benefit, it could well be for the good of a classmate or out-of-school friend.

Often, she would challenge herself to achieve something tricky, be it getting an extra few sherbet drops in her penny sweet bag in Mr Lavery's sweet shop or swiping a slice of P.C. Dawson's cake when he was standing talking at the end of his garden path. Sometimes for good measure, she would mix up all his paperwork relating to the cases that he should have been working on, a stolen bicycle, or a missing donkey. When he eventually drew breath and returned to his narrow, wobbly cheap wooden police desk, he would see the empty China plate and three-quarters drunk cold tea, and assume that he had eaten the cake, as he consumed so much cake, one slice just blurred into the next.

These behaviours came to Ida, almost subconsciously, as natural as blinking, she never thought about it afterwards, just carried on with her day. These misdeeds somehow never made their way back to Elmer or Maude, both of whom would have been hugely disappointed and angered with their surrogate daughter.

Her classmates were happy to be her friend, but were also slightly wary of her, sensing perhaps a slight unpredictability in her. Given her problematic start in life, she surprisingly possessed a healthy helping of emotional intelligence, this quality was not an attribute that her mother had been blessed with. Her school friends, at least the less adventurous ones, tended to head on home to their parents when they felt uneasy about what might happen next.

As Ida went about running errands, she would catch the elders of Marshcombe taking long surreptitious, sideways looks at her. Endeavouring to see if they could find a likeness to a fellow Marshcombe dweller. At the same time, apprehensive in the thought that any found likeness might be to their husband, uncle, or brother!

This habitual peering, rolled off her like ice cream of a hot stone, with her muttering to herself, 'Daft folk, they will bump into themselves if they don't look where they are going…ha ha ha.' Not once did Ida ever ask what they were gawking at, for she knew.

31

Janice was returning to her lodgings, sitting in a tired but happy enough daze on the last tram home. She had been out celebrating her workmate Varna's engagement to a boy called Terry. She was not drunk, just ebullient and starving hungry, thinking about the leftover rice pudding; she was going to wolf down with a big spoonful of blackcurrant jam when she got back in.

Staring out of the window, somewhat hypnotised by the trundle and rattle of the tram, she noticed a young woman walking in the direction that her tram had just come from. The woman, wearing a navy dress and red hat, had the exact same meandering way of walking as Sylvie. Snapped out of her "rice pudding" reverie, she stood up so sharply that her head felt like a spinning coin and banging on the window she yelled, 'Sylveee,' over and over again only sitting back down when she realised that the weary grey conductor was shouting at her, 'Missy, I won't tell you again—you be quiet this minute. That's enough carrying on, sit back down!'

Janice just could not be sure, as she sat down on her seat slightly stunned. Had it been Sylvie, it was her way of walking and the right height. But, in the summer darkness, really it could have been any young woman strolling home. Perhaps it was her subconscious that so dearly wanted it to be Sylvie? Had her imagination been fertilised by her drinking? Putting the key in the keyhole of her door she walked in and tiredly went to bed forgetting all about the cold rice pudding.

32

Of all the men in the Marshcome district, James Mumford was very high on the list of those who just wanted a steady, hard-toiling, rewarding passage through life. To pay his rent on time, on the "Quarter Days" of Christmas, Lady Day, Michaelmas and Midsummer Day. See to it that his cattle, sheep and horses were well tended to, and a few new healthy foals at the end of the spring.

He pondered as he forked fragrant fresh hay into the hay loft, what had he done in his fifty-eight years on God's earth to deserve such a despotic second wife? The consistently faithful Buster, a fine judge of human character despite his canine being, would have absolutely nothing to do with Rose, even if she was proffering a beef shin bone. As soon as he saw his master lay down his pudding spoon after the final mouthful of steamed treacle pudding and cream, the handsome dog was already sat by the back door, ready to be away from the huffing and groaning of the rotund keeper of his master. Rose was woefully un-self-aware that she was totally impervious to the depressing effects of her behaviour on her undemanding spouse and his steadfast hound.

Maude could see her father's marriage fraying at the edges causing him to become taciturn and the corners of his mouth constantly dropping. She hated to see this downcast demeanour in someone who had always been such a level-headed and cheerful man. At a loss as to what to do to help him, she most certainly was not going to tackle her stepmother on the subject. So, after discussing it with a thoroughly indifferent shrugging Elmer, she decided to gird her loins and visit him more often with Ida and spend the time with James amongst his dearly loved horses and Buster.

The following Saturday, on a sharpish March day, when their woollen vests had not yet been discarded, Ida and Maude cycled out to see James to cheer him up. As they approached Buckthorne Farm, a great cacophony of raised voices grew stronger. Rose, despite being a country dweller, was "giving out" to her husband in no uncertain terms that she thoroughly disapproved of him hanging a mare's afterbirth on a hawthorn hedge, by way of stockmen's superstition that this would ensure the health and long-term well-being of the foal.

'James, I'm not having it, that is repellent, not interested in your foolish folklore. Take it down this second.'

'No, I will not. I want that mare and her colt foal to thrive. What do you know about breeding horses eh? Will you just stop interfering woman? Never heard me telling you what to do with a Victoria sponge have you?'

This was all witnessed by the two visitors standing by their bicycles, their mouths gaping. Maude had seen her father do this for every foal born since she was small. It never did any harm, whether it did good who knew.

'I'm telling you again husband of mine, if you don't do as I ask…' Before she could finish her sentence, James who had now spotted Maude and Ida by the yard gate, dropped the wooden bucket he was holding, marched over to them, and said, 'Hello, my lovelies,' whilst taking Maude's bicycle from her, swinging his leg over and pedalling away towards the village.

Ida walked towards the unaccustomed dumb-struck Rose, 'Hello, Rose, any chance of a glass of milk, please?'

'If you must.'

Maude followed them into the kitchen where she attempted to engage the now sullen Rose in general chitchat, whilst Rose fetched a jug of milk from the slate shelf in the pantry. Ida sat down on a kitchen chair at the table, where she spotted Rose's new reading glasses. She discreetly took them out of the brown felt case. Then with thumbs and forefingers popped the lenses out, before replacing the glasses in the case, and putting the lenses in her coat pocket. She drank the milk as fast as her swallow reflex would allow and went outside.

Maude followed almost immediately, getting on Ida's bicycle, with her niece on the handlebars, they cycled back home. Very surreptitiously Ida was able to drop the two lenses onto the muddy road at the Green Lane junction, smiling slowly to herself as she did so. Later, whilst she ate her supper of beef brisket, mashed spuds, swede and carrots it did occur to her that now that her vile step-grandmother could not see to read, she would have considerably more time in which to aggravate her quiet life-seeking spouse. This Ida regretted but not the act.

33

Marjorie had not been without admirers since George's tragic but oh-so-timely tram tragedy. She had been out to the theatre with one or two men and had the odd afternoon tea engagements but was usually bored by the time the fruit scones were consumed. Yes, she certainly found them vaguely attractive, but something in her could just not really be bothered to invest the time and energy in these would-be suitors.

George had been indifferent between the sheets, very often content to check clients' balance sheets into the early hours. When the mattress did see some movement, it was brief and very often unapologetically a non-event. Leaving Marjorie to sort herself out during her morning bath. This lack of libido in her carefully chosen husband suited her well enough, as it was not George's high sex drive that had attracted Marjorie to him that day at the cinema entrance. His uses lay not under the eiderdown.

The few men who had tried to court her were always left feeling that they had a mountain to climb in getting to know the real Marjorie. Certainly, she was engaging enough, chatting about Eunice, Pico and, of course, her true passion was her emporium and naturally taking time to chat about their own work. But the men detected a façade, a deceptive outward-facing appearance that was troubling and puzzling. Birmingham was teeming with women who were puzzle-free and much less of a steep climb.

Marjorie had all she required, a thriving business in which her daughter could excel, her adored Pico, a very comfortable home on Francis Road and perfectly enjoyable sex on her own.

Divine's chatelaine thoroughly enjoyed seeing the girls who worked there, under her and Eunice's pinpoint scrutiny, flourish and develop into stylish, conversationally confident young women. All of whom could "hold their own" with any client who chose to walk through Divine's doors.

When Dina arrived in the immaculate showroom for her interview, she was far from the "finished product" as Marjorie referred to as her newest member of staff. In Dina, she saw a determined young woman with a sunny disposition, neither of them thinking that in time Dina would deputise for Eunice when she occasionally took a day out. Dina hailed from Nechells, a hard-pressed working-class area. Her Irish father worked all hours as a metal fabricator, and her mother was a domestic cleaner for the fierce Brian Fleming, a National Schools Inspector. At fourteen, Dina worked two jobs; before the crows were up, she was helping deliver milk and when that shift had finished her day began at Tulloch's shoe shop on Furnace Street. This six-days-a-week varied career path brought her to Divine's doors four years later.

Dina thrived and blossomed in the Divine bosom. Every morning throwing back the blankets and leaping out of bed, brimming with unbridled enthusiasm for her day ahead. Talking to varied and interesting people and challenging her sales skills, which after years on the shop floor at Tulloch's were as sharp as a drawing pin are what energised this young salesgirl! Only fifteen months younger than Eunice, she became somewhat of a confidant to the boss's daughter. On Eunice's more frustrating days, when she clashed with her mother over some element of the clothes display, or Marjorie's choice of poker game participants, Dina would share a sticky bun over a cup of tea in the upstairs kitchen, and soon have the conversation back to Roland and his shenanigans and hapless pursuit of Eunice.

As far as men were concerned Dina "wasn't especially bothered" as she said many times when the girls were chatting at closing time. She had huge admiration for her parents working as hard as they did. If she could give her mother Lilly a new coat or hat and gloves at Christmas, that really made her year.

None of Divine's girls were particularly set on marriage, despite that being the accepted social norm of the time. They had seen too many of their female relatives and friends in sorrowful marriages, with scant attention or respect from their bullish husbands. Overburdened with demanding, mewling children, with not a speck of time for themselves.

The Divine card evenings gained considerable popularity, necessitating a second evening a week being "soirée night". Eunice had mentioned the poker nights to Roland, and he in turn to his boss Edgar Bennett. Many of Birmingham's moneyed sporting gentlemen relied on Edgar to run their gambles. If there was a chance of alleviating the boredom of a long winter evening by the flic flac sound of cards being dealt then that and a malt whisky served by an attractive girl, well they were well in!

Roland, thinking that this information would elevate him in Edgar's eyes, which was not the case, left Roland contemplating what he could get out of these evenings. He thought long and hard but failed to see what benefit this brought him. Apart from perhaps a modicum of kudos from Eunice.

The girls were happy to work evenings, keen as they all were for that extra singing lesson, stylish new victory velour coat, or the latest T-strap heel shoes. Eunice and Marjorie would sit down together in the comfortable salon and work out the rota for the evenings. With daughter guiding the mother as to which one of the girls was "on their monthlies" and therefore would be happier not working.

Eunice felt the more popular the gaming nights became, there would be the need to find more girls to help out. As reluctant about this scenario as she was, she was well aware how well Dina, Martha, Lucy, and Peggy worked as a small team. She had witnessed bullying in her school and was wary of recruiting a potential "tricksy mare" to unbalance Divine's harmony. If one of the girls knew of a suitable candidate, then she would be happy to potentially give them a week's trial at work on the shop floor and in the salon.

34

Maude was not a woman of many words either verbally or on paper. But she had made every effort to write to Janice when she first moved to Birmingham, in the forlorn hope of hearing back that Janice had miraculously come across her Sylvie.

Janice was not a great letter writer but a reasonably enthusiastic scribbler of short notes and postcards. Most often including a page for Ida. She never mentioned Sylvie, only descriptions of her Sunday outings to Stratford-upon-Avon, and gossip about the other girls at the Midlands Vinegar factory. Neither did she mention her close-up and personal sticky encounter on the tram! Maude, on the prudish scale, was somewhere near the top.

After a good few years, Maude stopped writing to Janice as in all the letters she had sent, not once had she asked the question, 'Have you seen Sylvie?' This enquiry was just too painful to see in writing on the page. She never let on to Elmer that she had kept in touch with Janice, he, being of the opinion, that his sister-in-law had been the instrument of much worry and consternation when she had been around. Despite his charitable nature, he had no desire to see "his Maudie" further her stress and sadness over her errant sister. On less charitable days, he fell firmly into the "good riddance to bad rubbish" camp. This sentiment he kept very much to himself.

Sylvie's name was rarely mentioned between the two. Maude, however, when they were alone, made a point of talking freely to Ida about her mother as she was conscious that Ida should know something of Sylvie and their God-given similarities. Particularly, regarding their ears. Both of whom had a bit missing from the top of the left ear, as though a small rodent had nibbled on it, leaving the helix with a ragged edge.

Up until the age of ten Ida had an interest in Maude's recollections of Sylvie, but this faded to a benign irritation from then on. Ida would happily read the short scrawled pencilled notes from Janice to her but never asked Maude if there was news of her mother from Birmingham.

The seasons rolled on, from blue-filled skies to muddy and tiresome short days. P.C. Brian Dawson retired, much to the inhabitants of the Marshcombe's delight and relief, tired as they were of his ineptitude. With the more comedic members of the town commenting on the fact that P.C., Dawson would have even more time to eat cakes. He was replaced by a suitably eager beaver of a man by the name of P.C. Ted Gibbs. Who, in the first few months of his new posting, diligently cycled about his patch introducing himself, appearing to be efficient and hardworking. When Brenda Lockyer, the local midwife, offered him a slice of fruit loaf, he responded by saying, 'No, no, thank you, Mrs Lockyer, I have no time for cake on my rounds!'

Most of the locals welcomed this "new broom" sweeping clean their community. However, not Kipper! He felt the very opposite, seeing this new incumbent at the Police House as something of a hindrance to his way of making a living.

Perhaps this "new broom" was not as diligent as people had hoped. This Kipper felt was his only hope of continuing his unorthodox way of working and living.

Not one single resident of the Marshcombe Parish thought for a heartbeat that this shiny, new local copper would suddenly and curiously unveil the bewildering puzzle of Sylvie Mumford abandoning her daughter in a tin bath and vanishing…

Ida, encouraged by Mrs Noble and her aunt, began to make her own dresses, green and blue were her favourite colours. For Wilma's fifteenth birthday, she made her a maroon gingham pinafore dress which complimented her friend's barley sugar-coloured hair. Wilma loved it and it fitted her so well that she could not have been more delighted with a gift, promising Ida that she would always keep it even when, as she surely would, grow out of it.

Ida enjoyed the creative side of making clothes but was always a little bit impatient to finish the garment despite Mrs Noble's interjections of, 'Steady there Ida, slow it down, or you will be bound to make silly mistakes.'

When customers came in to collect their alterations or orders from the back of the workshop, Ida wondered what adventures these dresses would have with their wearers. But there again, she pondered, by looking at the majority of Grace Noble's customers, it was more than likely that the clothes would not have any at all.

Despite spending her spare time at a sewing machine, Ida still loved to career about the countryside on her much-pedalled bicycle or, as Elmer referred to it, 'That Ida running amok again.'

She was intensely aware that the opposite sex was interested in her and at the same time perhaps somewhat fascinated by her "couldn't give a biscuit" attitude. Maude, painfully aware of Ida's potentially problem-making elements in her niece's personality, began to fret and felt anxious on an almost weekly basis. If she tried getting Ida to sit down for just a minute and listen to her words of caution and basic moral guidance, Ida would jump up from her chair, pull her hair up into a knot and look to her aunt saying, 'I know, I know you all think I'm going to turn out a wrong'un.' Before Maude could put her lips together in response, her adoptive daughter was away on her blessed bicycle again.

35

Roland, with his evenings free and no Missus on the horizon, had pretty much-drawn stumps with Eunice and finally realised that he was punching way out of his league. He had it in his small head that he might make himself useful at Marjorie's Soirées. Perhaps bringing up fresh coal for the open fire in the bedazzling salon or helping with the gentlemen's coats. This he concluded, would be his only way "in" as playing cards was out of the question as he didn't know how! If Marjorie had known what he was thinking she would have choked on her whisky. Roland, aka Trevor, absolutely was not the sort of man she wished to have seated at her card tables.

Roland hovered in the ominous manner that was his norm at the end of Forde Street one autumn evening, taking extended noisy pulls on a soggy Woodbine. Eunice saw him sometime before he spotted her. Laughing to herself, she thought, *Feckin useless "lookout" he would make*. She was almost upon him when he noticed her, 'Oh, hello, Eunice, I was just having a fag. You all right?'

'Yes, I'm all right. Shouldn't I be now I have bumped into you?'

'Ha ha, you're a funny one, gal. Fancy a drink in the Tap Tavern?'

'No thanks, Roland, we have been very busy all day, I'm tired,' starting to walk off as she finished her sentence. He scuttled in his reptilian way in front of her, almost falling off the kerb as he did so and scuffing his boots. 'Any chance of you getting me in on these gaming nights at your place? After all, I did put the word out for you to Edgar and his cronies and associates.'

Thinking to herself as Roland spoke, 'There is about as much chance of my mother remarrying as of this one getting in on the card evenings!'

'Look, I will see about asking Mother, but you know what she is like. Bye.' With this, she set off down the pavement with an air of disdain. Laughing to herself at the contemplation of Roland in the salon, she would not mention it to her mother who would only laugh as long and hard as she was now doing.

The next day the shop was to be closed as Marjorie was giving the interior a "gladden up" as she called it, Eunice preferred calling it a "re-vamp". New maple glass display cabinets and exquisite full-length Chinoiserie styled mirrors were arranged with care. Along with two large, hammered brass umbrella stands with Fleur de Lys motifs. One of Eunice and Marjorie's absolute pet hates was dripping umbrellas; these new stands were so stunning that before long they became a much-used talking point, with Peggy quipping, 'Well, they will come in handy for stashing Mrs P's whisky hoard!' but not in earshot of Eunice.

Marjorie had the two delivery men position the heavy mirrors, then re-position them several times more before she was happy with their final resting place. By this time, the men had removed their brown "work" coats and raised their unruly bushy eyebrows a very many times! Finally, when they had gone, Eunice spent the afternoon carefully arranging lingerie and gloves on pale lilac tissue paper, happy that her mother was upstairs having her monthly manicure with the effervescent Clara.

Although Clara irritated Marjorie, she did do an excellent file and buff polish. The poor girl, desperate to chat about the latest styles, never got up a "head of steam" as Marjorie sat with one hand resting on Clara's the other holding a fashion magazine and scrutinising it intently. Almost baiting the poor girl who worked away head down until Marjorie's nails were shiny and immaculate.

Eunice was well aware of this veneer of titanium that her mother wore when someone or something annoyed her. She had witnessed this personality trait many times in her young life but had also seen her mother's nurturing side with both her and the girls who worked at Divine. Eunice had long given up trying to work out her mother's complex personality.

36

Married men made up the majority of those who frequented the evenings in Marjorie's elegant and sumptuous reception room, two of the regulars were single and three widowed in their fifties.

Initially, the card nights were most popular during the long gloom-filled mid-winter evenings, but as word spread, they became equally popular all year round; much to Marjorie's delight. "Evenings at D" as they became colloquially known were where men aged mid-thirties to late sixties of a healthy economic status went to enjoy themselves. The "guests" as the men were always referred to, were carefully and discretely vetted by Eunice and her mother, with the daughter responsible for the younger set. If they failed to meet Marjorie's stringent standards, they were not admitted principally based on their affluence.

Donald, Marjorie's dear friend when delivering flowers for the establishment, thoroughly enjoyed hearing how the nights had gone. Enthralled by the girls' loquacious and colourful descriptions of the guests.

'Oh, I don't know Stanley Tisman, never met him, but I know his wife, Merle; buys her blooms from me week in and week out.'

'Stanley is very amusing; never think he was headmaster of the Grammar School. Quite taken with our Lucy…' but before Peggy could continue, Marjorie sashayed into view, 'this tittle-tattling must stop Peggy this minute, go and tidy the gloves in the store cupboard. Come on Donald, come and have a pot of tea with me upstairs where we can gossip all we like.'

Upstairs the conversation was less scuttlebutt and more reminiscent of an information-gathering exercise by Marjorie. Donald, having lived all his sixty-four years in Birmingham, knew a great many people from all walks of life. He may not have known all these people well, but he had the capability to find out a good deal about them. Gladly depositing these gems of information into Marjorie's scented lap. He was only too happy to keep on the "right side" of Marjorie, deducing very early on in their friendship, that having her as a foe was not a wise move.

Donald was fond of all the girls and grateful for the way they embraced his "particular penchant", and he would tell Marjorie so when they had their chats.

Very often the teapot was abandoned in favour of glasses of whisky if Donald's information was particularly tantalising. Swishing from the drinks cabinet and placing a generous Laphroaig whisky in her good friend's expectant hand, she would say, 'Dear Donald, thank you for that. The quality of my girls will always be recalled, but the cost is forgotten.' Smiling wryly as she spoke.

From as soon as Marjorie could recall, she had an innate ability to wheedle out and identify a man's vulnerability; she knew not where this came from, but it was exceedingly useful! She rolled with it, enhancing, and finessing this skill as she matured. This trait was not acquired from her poor subjugated and ground-down Mother, who, since Marjorie's retail ascendancy, had ensured she had received a generous monthly handout.

37

Some of the younger lads employed at Durent's racing yard, including the irrepressible young Jonjo, made up the group that Ida considered her friends, outside of school.

Wilma was really only content to latch onto Ida when it was just the two of them, not having the confidence to banter with the leery yard lads and "want to be jockeys".

Jonjo and Ida had been firm and consistent friends from the moment that they became neighbours. Of course, he had heard the ceaseless tittle-tattling of his elders for years. Before he was taken on as an apprentice, he had accompanied his father Paul to the yard in school holidays and, on Saturdays, keen to fill water buckets and to fork up clean, crisp wheat straw for the racehorses' luxuriant bedding so had been party to all the chitchat. Enthusiastic to make a good impression with the head lad Samuel.

Most of the gossip was exchanged when the stable staff sat warming their numbing chilled hands and feet, nursing chilblains, squashed up together on wooden benches around the small coal burner after their second cold gallop of the morning—gloves were something that only ladies and toffs wore! So Jonjo just listened and watched, subconsciously scanning the faces and mannerisms of the older men, in the wood-panelled horse sweat-smelling room, for similarities to his fervent friend Ida.

One late afternoon in his last year at school, after the Marshcombe Spring Fair, Jonjo had got his hands on two bottles of Marston Stout. He disliked the taste but enjoyed the effect, so he persevered with both bottles. Not long after dispatching the second one and chucking it over the laurel hedge of Mr Raddock the undertaker's back garden with exaggerated aplomb, he came across Ida cycling and stuffing back a large piece of fruit loaf smothered in butter, the larger part of her face covered in melting butter. His friend came abruptly to a halt when she spied Jonjo lurching about on the track.

'Hello J, you look "beery". What you been up to?'

'Swiped a couple of bottles out of a wooden crate…' The words stopped suddenly, as though standing was consuming all his mental and physical capacity at that particular moment in time.

'Whose crate?' Ida asked.

After some delay by which time Ida was beginning to lose interest, Jonjo finally responded slowly, 'Er, err, the crate at the back of the beer tent, no one looking I reckoned.'

'Ha ha, well, you would be in a hell of trouble if anyone did see you! Come on let's go and scratch our initials in the Shipton Road bus shelter; we haven't done that one yet!'

The pair of them wobbled on Ida's bicycle over to the bus shelter, narrowly avoiding a mishap when Jonjo started waving his arms around. With his penknife, they hacked determinedly into the left-hand wooden upright post leaving a very obvious "IM" and "JD" in the wood.

Jonjo appeared to be sobering up and suggested that they went to look around "old man Raddock's" outbuilding and check out any dead 'uns.

As they were making their way back towards Marshcombe, Ida thought that she saw something moving under a line of willow trees in Tom Smedley's top field. They leapt off the bicycle leaving it capsized in the long grass and made their way into the field. Walking quietly abreast towards the movements that Ida had seen from the road. As they got closer, Jonjo indicated to Ida to squat down low, as they did, it was obvious to the both of them that they had stumbled upon Kipper Brown, identifiable by the bright red braces that he always wore which were wrapped around his ankles along with his corduroy trousers and worn out under shorts.

It was all Jonjo and Ida could do to keep quiet, bursting at the seams as they were with uncontrollable laughter and made all the more entertaining when Kipper's bare backside began rhythmically imitating a piston! They could make out a recipient of this enthusiastic rutting but could only see her coal-black coloured hair and pale green dress pulled up to her shoulders, pretty much smothering her face. Judging by the appreciative hollering of the beneficiary, Kipper was clearly doing a most proficient job!

The two puce-faced teenage gigglers retreated quietly back to the track, slumping down in the grass wailing like banshees.

'Do you think we could do that Ida?'

This direct question set Ida off laughing again.

'No chance with you, J.J. I like boys taller than you. Who do you reckon that was under Kipper? John Caper's Missus maybe?'

'Kip is like a travelling dog fox, don't know who it was, don't care, not bothered.'

'But if we could work out who it was, might be useful don't you reckon?'

'Maybe, but my head's raging. C'mon give me a lift and let's get home or Elmer, and my da will be on our case.'

After a supper of baked potatoes with hunks of cheese and Maude's green bean chutney, Ida lay on the bed in her small room above the pantry. Mulling over the notion of having sex, something she was thoroughly accustomed to having grown up surrounded by farm animals from a young age.

She arrived at the conclusion that if she was going to have sex, it would not be in a damp field with her clothes pulled up to her neck and elbows "nettle stung" to hell with grass burn knees. With that thought, she undressed, pulled on her nightgown and leapt into bed, promptly falling into a deep slumber till morning.

38

Both Maude and Grace Noble had hoped dearly that Ida would pursue work in the dressmaking profession, as she was clearly talented and had gained plenty of experience under Grace's hawk eyes and meticulous mentoring.

At some point during the Christmas break in Ida's last year in school, she emphatically declared one lunchtime, over a warming bowl of leek and potato soup, to Elmer and Maude that she wanted to join the Royal Mail.

'What on earth makes you want to do that Ida?' a surprised Elmer asked.

'I like the uniform. Have you seen what the women wear, Maudie?'

'Er no, I haven't. Bert Mitchell is Marshcombe's postie, and he wears dull old garb.'

'Well, I'm telling you, I have seen pictures in the *Birmingham Post* and those girls wear a blue serge skirt, peak slouch cap and a waterproof cape when it rains; ever so smart.'

'Now steady down, you might change your mind come the end of school in the summer. You would have no lodgings and not know a soul.'

'But Maudie, I would, I could write to Janice. She would be sure to help us.'

A decidedly anxious Maude, who had known that something along these lines was heading their way, swiftly changed the subject to Durent's Christmas Eve party, an event which was always popular with the youngsters.

39

School was out and Ida was happy to take her final cycle ride from the school to the cottage where she slung her workbooks onto the dresser with such fervour that Maude's crockery jangled alarmingly. Ida was set; her mind was not for turning. No amount of Maudie's cautionary, diffident, discouraging words would sway her otherwise; it was Birmingham for her.

Some large part of Maude still saw her adoptive daughter as the little snuffling mite, squatting and shivering in that tepid tin bath. Somehow not being Ida's biological mother seemed to dilute her parental authority. During one protracted scene of door slamming during which Ida would not have been out of place in any London theatre farce production, an exasperated Maude sank down into Elmer's carver chair.

'Ida please, please, just think for a minute. Mrs Noble has said many a time that she would employ you full-time. Your home is here with Elmer and me for life.'

'I'm going Maudie, you and Elmer won't be stopping me. You know I will visit when I get some holiday due. You know it is all arranged with the Royal Mail and Janice sent a picture postcard saying I can stop with her, so I am all sorted. See, nothing to worry about.'

Maude sat twisting the bottom corner of her hessian-coloured apron, almost paralysed by the thought of Ida stepping out into the bright, busy world that she had never been bold enough to sample.

None of Ida's forceful statements of her leaving filled Maude with any sort of reassurance or confidence. However, she felt a kernel of assurance that there was an innate sense of worldliness in her "little bean" despite her simple agricultural upbringing and lack of broadened horizons. She did not know where this came from. Many an incredulous Marshcombe resident had been heard to say over the years how "knowing" that young Ida was.

Only Jonjo's brimming glass full of ebullient personality swayed him from being downcast at the prospect of his best friend flying the coop. He too, like Maude, knew it would surely come to this. All she ever talked about during their adventures together was leaving "Drudgetown" behind her.

'Nothing here for me J.J.,' Ida had told him.

On her last weekend, the pair of them cycled over to Luscombe Downe, leaving their cycles at the bottom of the Iron Age Fort. Both soon beady with sweat as they reached the top slumping down in the sheep nibbled summer's end stubby grass that prickled through their thin clothes. As they lay side by side in contented silence, the still July day sizzled their skins.

'Going to miss you, Ida. It will be very boring without you. Will you come watch me if I get to race ride at Birmingham? Please say you will.'

'Course, I will J.J. You numbskull, you know I will.'

Jonjo, utterly focused on his life path, his drive to succeed as a jockey knew no bounds. Working his way up through the ranks at Durent's would surely pay off if he grafted hard enough. Whilst doing tedious yard jobs such as forking up the muck cart or scrubbing feed buckets, he would often daydream of swaggering about in fine tweed clothes and handmade boots; the bounty of making it as a successful jockey.

He understood his feisty friend's desire to shed the conformist cloak that engulfed her.

Then as the two of them lay soporifically, Ida suddenly and silently pulled herself up onto one elbow and leaning over Jonjo, set a long sensual kiss on his unexpecting but most willing lips. Their tongues mingled like cocaine-fuelled eels for some moments with saliva and sweat from their top lips merging until Ida jumped up.

'That's my goodbye to you, J.J.'

'Oh, please come back down here, please. I want you.'

'C'mon get up you lazy arse of a boy and get rid of the cucumber! That is all you are getting from me.' Laughing hard she began to walk back down the steep incline. As he continued to sit looking stupefied and grinning, she shouted over her shoulder crowing as she ran, 'Race you back, if you win you might get a winner's kiss!'

40

On a dun-coloured morning, James Mumford had ridden his favourite retired horse Golden Tower, so named because his coat was a burnished orange and he was some seventeen hands high, over to say his farewell to Ida a few days before her much argued upon departure.

Folk rarely visited him; most having been verbally scalded one too many times by the pernicious Rose. Buster had long since gone to the rainbow bridge; James had not replaced him, having no need for a guard dog now for he had his wife!

Ida was greatly fond of her grandfather. Many nights she had lain in her narrow bed, with her eyes crunched closed, willing Rose to fall into the Teversham's lake and sink slowly, silently, and leadenly to the murky bottom. Her "granda" had changed greatly during his ill-advised union; gone was his cheery personality, replaced by morose apathy.

He had not opposed Ida's leaving in any great way. Having told her many times that she should do what makes her content and that if she was in any difficulty, she must write to him, and he would help her in any way he could. His ears were closed long ago to his wife's heart-piercing persistent utterances about Ida's overconfidence and wilfulness. He had a sense that those traits would take Ida as far as she wanted to go.

Maude, her father, and Ida drank big cups of tea with homemade Eccles cakes around the kitchen table. Eventually, James stood up, 'Come here, my girl,' he said giving his granddaughter a lengthy bear hug.

'Good luck, Ida, you make sure you write our Maudie regular now,' whilst pressing a pound note into her right hand.

Maude had seen to it that Ida had four new dresses, two summer ones and two for winter. All were beautifully made by herself, and the materials were given by Mrs Noble. A new nightdress and two woollen tops, one cream and one blue with the latest puff sleeves, much to Ida's glee, completed her new wardrobe.

Ida knew the most difficult goodbye would be with Wilma. She had even contemplated not saying goodbye at all, but Maude had shut that thought down sharply. They had remained friends in the last year of school, but in truth, Ida had felt irritated by her friend's neediness and lack of ambition.

After a long wait at Wilma's backdoor, during which Ida thought, *They are not home—good.* The door was snatched open by a flushed face Wilma who threw her arms around Ida's neck, almost throttling her in her distress, leaving Ida's neck damp with snot and plentiful tears.

'Idee, please stay.' Even this childhood nickname irked her now.

'Chin up, Wilma, I am not going to the moon, only to Birmingham! Nothing to snivel about. You could have made plans to go too.'

As she said this, she crossed her fingers. She had no intention of her new life being shackled by Wilma's inhibitions and well-held anxieties.

'Just think how happy your folk will be to see the back of me!' she chortled.

Wilma stood sniffing as Ida gave her a brief hug, doing her best to avoid the abundance of snot.

The following morning Ida, decked out in one of her new summer dresses, leapt on board the bus. Elmer had placed her suitcase in the baggage section for her after giving her a kiss on the forehead and a fiver into her handbag. The bus driver made much of shouting, somewhat unnecessarily as there were only five passengers, 'All on, all on leaving now!'

Ida climbed aboard and sat down putting her coat and bag neatly on the empty seat beside her. Maude and Elmer stood waving metronomically like sad puppets, Maude's cheeks damp from tears. They waved until the bus was long out of sight.

As the bus drove away from the village, a sense of liberation came over Ida, along with a beaming smile. She had not thought about what to expect, but she was self-assured beyond her years, and she had achieved the first part of her life's journey in leaving Marshcombe, equipped with self-belief, tenacity, and a burgeoning awareness of her profound potency over the male species.

In the past five years or so, Sylvie was rarely mentioned in the Mumford family. Maude would have dearly loved to talk about her much-missed sister; she could see that mention of her to her father only compounded his misery. Elmer had long ago stated in his quiet emphatic way that there would be no more talk "of that one in the cottage".

Ida's desire to find a job in Birmingham kindled the thought in Maude that her "little bean" was subconsciously seeking her mother. However, Maude never discussed this brewing assumption with "her little bean". She had long stopped enticing Ida to talk about her mother, fearful of Ida's cheerful positivity and self-containment abandoning her.

41

Birmingham was something of an enormous jolt to Ida's whole being. As the bus made its way through the city, the endless cacophony of sounds, fumes and chimney soot and dirt that abounded the streets, rendered her awestruck.

Janice had suggested in her last letter that Ida take the Saturday morning bus from Marshcombe in order that she could meet her off the bus at the Digbeth Terminus. Descending from the bus with her mouth opened so wide it might have held an imaginary cooking apple, only closing it when Janice gave her a vast breath-stopping bosomed hug.

'Look at you, Ida! Not Maudie's "Little Bean" no more! You are rightly a corker girl.'

'Come on, let's get you a cuppa and a sarnie in Bill's café.' Off they went with Ida, one hand carrying her new suitcase, the other holding Janice's hand which they cheerily swung back and forth.

Janice now rented a couple of rooms at the top of a tired-looking house in Paxton Street. The living space had a largish southwest-facing double window overlooking the backyard which she opened wide on warm sunny days; not that she was there very much what with the long shifts at the factory and some fierce socialising. She had made it homely enough; the best she could. The wooden floors had a few rag rugs bought from the market which afforded some protection from the pesky and persistent splinters.

A decrepit wrought iron single bed that complained so loudly when she turned over; it was always a cheery surprise each morning that it had not collapsed under her whilst she slept! The bed would have definitely not withstood any "barney mugging", not that Janice could have successfully smuggled a fella past her landlady.

There was a lumpy, wiry horsehair couch which was set to be Ida's bed for the foreseeable future. Janice had a gas ring for kettle boiling; she never ever did any cooking, taking her meals in the cafes and tea rooms as well as the plentiful canteen at work where there was always hearty hot fare on offer.

The only fly in the ointment of this vaguely homely setup was sinewy Mrs Pritchard the widowed, pious, and mealy-mouthed landlady. Left in borderline penury after Gordon, her gambling-addicted husband threw himself in the Grand Union Canal. Mr Pritchard had returned from the First World War, suffering terrible depression, and had shown signs of extreme psychological distress. Partially alleviated by a crippling addiction to gambling. The gambling and depression had won the unequal struggle, with the Grand Union Canal claiming him on a miserable February afternoon. Emily Pritchard felt permanently peeved by her compulsory need to take in lodgers.

Janice would give herself an imaginary pat on the back if she made it from opening the peeling painted front door, wiping her boots on the jute mat, and getting to the first landing without encountering Mrs "So Peeved" as Janice relished in calling her!

Janice spent the day after Ida's arrival showing her some of the city. This brought forth more and more mouth gaping and a great many questions from Ida. Amongst Janice's "Life in Birmingham" advice was "Never catch the eye of a man on the street, bus or tram". This gem was partially based on her own early days flashing experience, not that she had looked him in the eye! 'If a fella offers to buy you a tea, accept (prudent economics) drink it, tell him nothing about yourself and scarper.'

Ida was astonished by the vast volume of people; on the pavements, crossing roads, in parks and shops. By the end of her first day exploring the city, she fell into a fitful sleep.

On Monday morning, she duly reported for work at the Central Sorting Office, where she was engaged in a three-month probation period. Initially, mail sorting, before a further trial period "on the box" delivering letters.

Firstly, was an "eyeing up" by Mrs Lambert, the women's supervisor, who was reed thin and sported a very impressive lisp and a hacking persistent cough. Ida initially found this equally amusing and irritating. Mrs Lambert appeared with the much-longed-for uniform for Ida to try on in the curtained cubicle in the women's restroom. The blue serge skirt she had so looked forward to was heavy and worst of all, itchy, which made her think of Kipper's victims amongst the nettled field. But she had not one iota of intention of failing and returning to the bosom of Marshcombe unsuccessful.

42

Despite being reasonably self-aware, Ida had not accounted for her extremely low boredom threshold. The work was utterly mind-numbingly repetitive and dull. Any chance of not pulling her weight was scuppered by Mrs Lambert's hawk-like eyes monitoring her every move; before a firm tap on her left shoulder and the inevitable monotone, 'Ida, remember what I said, concentrate at all times.'

At this point, Ida was most often in a reverie, back in Marshcombe bantering with Jonjo and not thinking about letters bound for Scotland or Suffolk. The uniform was thoroughly disappointing, hot, scratchy, and not in the least bit flattering. *No chance of free cuppas in this dreary garb*, Ida thought to herself.

In school, she made friends freely. In their breaks, the women sat in the designated female-only restroom, a long rectangular room with wooden lockers hugging the walls and benches down the centre. They shared tales of their Saturday evenings out in the Glassmakers Arms and general workplace gossip. Fortunately, beady-eyed Mrs Lambert had herself a tiny office which she brewed up in, before buffing the brass plaque on the door denoting her the women's supervisor.

The new recruit absorbed everything like a mossy lawn. The majority of her co-workers were city-born and bred. Ida asked a great many questions which they never seemed to tire of.

'What were the Digbeth baths like?'

'Are there any good-looking boys in the sorting office?'

'Where can I buy a cheap pair of gloves?'

Vera, who had worked there for almost three years, eagerly answered all of Ida's questions. The girls lived for their weekends. Often after a lie-in, a delicious luxury even on a lumpy couch after starting at 6:00 a.m. each weekday, Ida would persuade Janice to come swimming with her and Vera, who she had promised to teach how to swim. Vera could not have been more different from Wilma, outgoing and spirited with bounteous creamy blonde hair and almond-shaped grey eyes. She had a wonderful infectious loud laugh. Ida enjoyed listening to her chatter away about her exploits with the "bozos" as she called young men.

'Just you wait Ida I'm going to catch myself a wealthy fella, with decent bricks and mortar and tidy teeth!'

Taken aback as Ida was by the lengthy signage on entering the baths of rules and regulations, no skinny dipping here she giggled to herself, it was good to be doing something she loved. Vera proved an able student, and after just a few Saturday afternoon sessions, she was making a decent impression of a graceful breaststroke across the pool's width. The girls usually followed this with a pot of tea and tea cakes with jam at Butters Tea House.

After the initial shock of the busyness of Birmingham, Ida settled into her new life, even mastering dodging a tram fare or two!

Janice had given her all the tools she needed to thrive in her new life. But after five weeks of her lodger arriving, Janice began courting a rakish-looking lean man called Desmond Calder who worked as a yard foreman at a builders' merchant. So, Ida spent less of her spare time with her mother's friend. This did not bother her; if she wasn't meeting Vera, she was entirely happy amusing herself with the contents of Janice's make-up bag and trying on her clothes or exploring Cannon Hill Park; *although not quite as lovely as the meadows and lanes of Marshcombe*, she thought.

As promised, Ida wrote to Maude once a week, usually on a Sunday evening with her week's news. Omitting fare dodging and pinching apples off the fruit stall in Hockley Market, also failing to mention how much she hated the sorting office, and it was possibly the dreariest job on the planet.

What she did write of was how hard she worked, how well Janice minded her and how well she was taking care of herself. She had no intention of Maude fretting herself daft. She always asked after her granda, never mentioning the despised Rose. On one of her meanders about the city, she had bought a postcard of Ard Patrick, the winner of the 1902 Epsom Derby, from a small kiosk to send to him. In her small, neat writing she asked after the horses and hoped he was well. Maude replied that her father had pinned the postcard to the mantle in his tack room, a place where he spent much of his time alone.

43

Ida's probation period flew by; numbed by the tedium of the working day, she was mightily relieved to have got to the end of it. Mrs Lambert summoned her into her terrifyingly tidy office on a Friday morning. Paper and pencil lay equally spaced in the centre of the woodworm-infested table that masqueraded as a desk.

'Well, Ida, to say that I am surprised is an understatement. Never did I think for a minute on your first day here that you would stay the distance. Clearly, you are not destined for a gold watch! I think we are both aware that perhaps your distinct personality is wasted here in the Midlands Central Sorting Office.'

'Thank you, I understand, Mrs Lambert. Are you letting me go?'

Ida was standing in front of the worm-holed desk with her hands clasped tightly behind her back, something she did when endeavouring to curb her irritation. She sure as hell was not going to leave on this shrew of a woman's say so, and not before she had found herself another job.

'No, Ida, you are staying on for the foreseeable future, but rest assured that I will be continuing to monitor your work.'

'Oh, thank you, Mrs Lambert. I will be here for my next shift bright and sharp,' she said trying as hard as she might not to impart the sarcasm and disrespect that was brimming within her.

As she left the office, she turned around very slowly and gave the closed door "the finger" muttering into her chest "swing on it".

Walking back to Janice's digs, after hopping off the No. 47 tram, she couldn't understand how Vera could have been stuck for three years in that dull place. She began laughing at how; when she was back in Marshcombe, she had longed to work there, even dreamt about it!

After a large bowl of rather chewy mutton stew in Casey's Cafe, she flopped, fully clothed, onto the basic single bed that she and Janice had sourced in the thrift shop on Hockley Road and instantaneously fell into a deep slumber.

To perk herself up, Ida spent the latter part of Saturday morning that week at the swimming baths. Swimming brought her joy and solace. As she swam, a young athletic woman in a very fetching navy and cream striped bathing costume strode commandingly down the steps into the rippling water and slid through the pool like an eel. *Impressive swimming*, Ida thought. After half an hour or so, she got out and went to her changing cubicle, followed shortly by the object of her admiration.

Both changed readily and emerged into the hall at the same time. As Ida was putting her swim bag on her shoulder, she heard the young woman say, 'You are a good and strong swimmer; where did you learn?'

Ida turned, buoyed by the woman's compliments.

'Oh, thank you, I learnt in the lake near my hometown of Marshcombe. I love swimming, it makes me happy it does.'

'Do you fancy a cuppa? Sorry, I am Eunice, and you are?'

Introductions complete, and Janice's words of wisdom forever ringing in her ears, 'Never turn down a free cuppa.' The two of them set about walking to a tea house that Eunice knew, where they made beltingly good tea cakes.

Bonding as they did over their mutual enjoyment of swimming, they chatted freely for almost an hour. Eunice learnt that Ida hated her postal work job and that this attractive, confident girl was utterly wasted in that sphere.

Ida gleaned that Eunice was a young woman who had beautiful clothes and was someone she felt instinctively that she must get to know. They agreed to meet up and swim together the following week.

44

Janice was fully intending to get Desmond to put a ring on her finger. She was hurtling into spinsterhood and felt that her options were fast running out. These impending nuptial plans were not lost on Ida who was well aware that she might be needing alternative digs. For Janice, a phantom pregnancy was soon conjured up, and Desmond was snared.

Ida thought all week as to how she might impress Eunice. Little did she realise that she already had. They met at the ticket kiosk just inside the women's entrance of the swimming pool, paid their dues and were soon displaying stylish breaststrokes in unison, occasionally pausing at the pool ends to chat.

After a Bakewell tart and a pot of tea in Lyons Tea House, which Eunice paid for, she suggested that Ida might like to call into Divine after her Tuesday shift as she would very much like her mother to meet her.

The following Monday after work, Ida made her way to Forde Street and very slowly walked past Divine's bedazzling double-fronted shop façade. Then crossing the road, she slowly walked past again, enchanted by the pale blue themed window dressing, which was enhanced with ostrich feathers and hand-painted paper clouds suspended from the ceiling, above elegant evening dresses. This is where Eunice works? Ida marvelled she must be the real deal!

The following day she put her best dress into a bag, changing into it after her shift, brushed her thick hair vigorously, clipping it up with two tortoiseshell clips that Janice had lent her. Dabbed some rouge on her cheeks and applied some muted pink lipstick.

Divine's door was heavy and not long freshly painted, Ida thought as she slightly apprehensively entered this other world. She was no sooner inside when Peggy sashayed towards her.

'Oh, hello, Ida. You must be here to see Marjorie Peyton. I am Peggy,' offering her right hand as she spoke.

Blimey was all Ida could think; she was properly formal.

Seated upstairs in the kitchen she could hear women's voices in the room next door. After a few minutes, much to Ida's relief, Eunice appeared.

'Ah, excellent there you are Ida, come on into the salon and meet my mother.' *What on earth is a "salon"?* Ida thought. Sitting at the fanciest desk, she had ever seen was her potential new employer; she gave this grand, well-dressed lady her best smile.

'Good afternoon, Ida. Eunice has told me a good deal about you. Do you think you would like to work here at Divine?'

'Yes, Mrs Peyton, I would like that very much! I am desperate to leave the sorting office.'

Marjorie then asked Ida, 'How old are you, my dear?'

'Just gone sixteen, Mrs Peyton.'

'Well, Ida, let me and Eunice have a talk. You wait downstairs in the back hallway for a few minutes.'

Ida skipped down the stairs and did as she was asked.

'Well, mother, what do you think,' asked Eunice.

'You were right to bring her. She has definitely got something, but she is "in the rough". You will have to put in a good bit of time with her to get any sort of polish on her.'

'I'm prepared to do that; she is bright and eager to learn. I will have that rustic and rural manner off her in a jiffy.'

'All right then, if you are busy put her under Lucy's wing and for goodness sake get her a decent haircut and a manicure. She has hands like a farm girl and also work on her accent and walk.'

Eunice found Ida sitting on the bottom of the stairs looking at her hands. 'Ida, you better give your notice to your Mrs Lambert. Just to start with you will help out generally, before we let you loose on the shop floor! Come on through and meet the other girls.'

Ida, so elated as she left Divine, quickly walked the whole way back to Janice's, bursting to tell her of her new job and the wonder of such a sparkling and elegant new workplace.

After about an hour, although it seemed longer to Janice, Ida finally drew breath and sat down, having regaled her with the delights of Divine's interiors, the fabulous dresses, and her new workmates. Of course, the pair of them had seen Divine from the No. 9 tram as it trundled down Forde Street. But never did they imagine for a fleeting second that either of them would ever venture into the inner sanctum of such a wonderful store.

'Well, girly, sounds like we are both finally making some progress with our lives. My "pregnancy" has worked a treat! Desmond and I are set to wed a week Saturday, just two days before my "miscarriage". He has a nice enough place on

Coppard Street, well it will do when I fix it up a bit,' she finished with a long-exaggerated wink.

'I'm real pleased for you, Janice.'

'Right now, I had better go and talk to Pritchard. Do you want to take these rooms on when I go if she agrees?'

'Yes, I'm promised better money and bumper tips if I serve at the card games. It will save me from searching for somewhere else. Tell the old crow I will be staying on till I find a better place, just don't tell her that bit!'

The days could not go fast enough for Ida, serving out her notice and listening to Mrs Lambert tutting was hellish. This was only interspersed with Janice's non-cvent of a wedding, the guests consisted of a witness, Frank, a work colleague of the lucky groom, Ida and two of Janice's friends Molly and Ellie from the Vinegar Factory. The formalities completed they celebrated in the Hawkspear Inn until closing.

The day eventually came when Ida left the job that she had so looked forward to back in Marshcombe. A broad grin appeared as she folded up the prickly uniform and left it in her locker.

45

Ida woke abruptly at 4:30 in the morning on the day she was due to start at Divine. Then suddenly, she remembered with a jolt that she did not have to be there until nine. Nine in the morning, surely the best part of the day gone as she recalled her granda saying.

Failing to go back to sleep and fearful of oversleeping, she washed and dressed in her better winter dress, coat and hat and took herself for a walk to settle her nerves. After a bowl of porridge and a big mug of sweet tea at Bob's Café, she made her way with nervous excitement to her new job.

The other girls were already there hanging up their coats in the back hallway. Marjorie never in until sometime later and Eunice had not yet arrived.

'Morning, Ida, let me show you around before we open up,' Lucy offered perkily.

Ida obediently followed her upstairs for a tour of the salon which she now understood to be where the card evenings were held.

'I don't know how to play cards, Lucy.'

Laughing through her words, 'No, no, Ida, you don't get to play cards, the guests and Mrs Peyton play, never us girls.'

'Oh, well that's a relief then.' Just as the tour was set to continue, Martha called up the stairs needing some help with a missing receipt.

Once in the shop itself Dina, who had been very friendly and chatty when Ida had come for her interview such as it was, took her into the storeroom where stocks of smaller items such as gloves, lingerie, scarves and shoes sat in orderly contentment on racks waiting for their new owners. At the far end, neatly stacked away were various props, pieces of furniture, dried flowers, paint pots and all manner of things ready for Eunice to work her creative magic when dressing the windows.

Next Martha took Ida back upstairs and showed her the tea-making routine.

'The gilt tray over there is only for Mrs P's use, and she has her tea strong, supped from this delicate tea set. Oh, and don't get caught calling her Mrs P, I only do it when I know I can get away with it!'

'Thank you, Martha, I understand. Can you tell me more about the card evenings that I also have to help out at?'

'That will be for Eunice to explain to you. Do you know how to be around moneyed, intoxicated men Ida? That is what you need to know.'

'Well, never been around moneyed sorts, not where I come from. They are mostly beer and cider-drinking hedge monkeys!'

'Us girls will sort you out on your first evening helping, just watch one of us.'

Eunice appeared in a chic plum-coloured dress and matching shoes.

'Right now, Ida, get your coat and hat, we need to get you buffed and gussied up.'

As they walked along the pavement, Eunice began to address the way Ida walked, which resembled, in her eyes, a sailor on shore leave and late back to his ship.

'Never ever look as though you are in a hurry, even if you are. Lift your head, drop your shoulders back and move your hips slightly forward. Now slow the walk right down, no slower than that.'

All these instructions gave Ida a headache. Despite walking a good deal slower, she felt as though she might fall flat on her face. The walking task was partly accomplished. Ida relaxed a bit and enjoyed the process of having her hair cut and re-styled. During this, Eunice endeavoured to work on her new recruit's bucolic pronunciation.

Marjorie had asked Ida to bring her a tea tray at 3:00 and seemed pleased with Ida's slightly more à la mode presentation. Once Ida had set the gilt tray on the occasional table, Marjorie said, 'Now, Ida, I would like you to take off your pinafore apron and walk up and down the salon a few times.'

This she did, trying very hard to do as she had been instructed that morning by Eunice.

'Not bad, Ida, a great improvement in a very short time. Keep working at it and it will become second nature in no time.'

On her journey home, Ida was taken aback at how thoroughly kind and helpful the girls had been, they seemed genuinely pleased to have her there. Confident from an early age, this scenario had edged her into unknown territory, but the words of encouragement only confirmed her conviction to succeed. She couldn't wait to meet Vera at the weekend and tell her all about it.

46

Letter writing had fallen hard and fast amongst Ida's list of priorities, but she did make herself write a most reassuring page and a half to Maude. Detailing her exciting new position at the luxury gown shop, the new sensible friends she was going to make there, and a very great deal about Eunice and somewhat less, as she knew very little about her impressive new employer, Marjorie Peyton.

However, her aunt remained none the wiser with regards to Janice moving out of Mrs Pritchard's house, and the card evenings in Divine's salon.

Ida heard back by return which she had anticipated. Very little had changed in Marshcombe and the surrounding villages. There was no news of Jonjo, Wilma was working at Ruffords, the shoe shop, and Elmer had a bad go with a gout attack. Of course, her aunt was most keen to know when Ida was coming home for a visit. Fortunately for Ida, it would not have occurred to Maude to fetch up in Birmingham such an excursion would be considered far too outlandish to Maude, her self-confidence not stretching to such a visit. This fact Ida had been fairly confident of when she had sat down on the bus that Saturday morning many months before.

Eunice had given Ida some "home practice" as she referred to it. Concentrating on her improved walk and the pronunciation of certain words all of which she had written in a small notebook. She thought this would be easy, but it was harder than she had envisaged. For a start, there was very little room in her digs, so she worked on her walking in the parks, strangely not remotely self-conscious whilst practising her less than "daughter of the soil" accent and mastering her refined walk. All the while hoping one day she might sashay into a room, as the other Divine girls did so wonderfully.

True to her instruction, Lucy took Ida under her wing. When Eunice gave her protégé a few of her old dresses, it was Lucy who guided Ida in how to style them, what colours worked best together and how to pin a hat at just the right and fashionable jaunty angle.

At the start, the days seemed to fly by despite spending most of her time observing the team and Eunice attending to customers. Shoppers were not served; they were "seen to" or "attended to".

Eunice talked Ida through the many styles, and a myriad of outfits for every social occasion, Mother of the Bride, Honeymoon, Tea Dresses, Formal Luncheons and Dinners and Evening Gowns.

Ida proved Eunice correct. She was sharp and eager to do well, as could be said for all four of the other girls. But, despite this there was not a snippet of competitiveness or jealousy amongst them, that being something simply not tolerated by Eunice or her mother.

After her first month, a small well-to-do lady in her sixties who walked with a stick came in to buy some cream leather button-backed gloves. Peggy suggested that Ida serve her.

'Good afternoon. I am Ida. How may I help you, Madam?'

'I am on the hunt for a fine pair of leather gloves, and I know that I must be in the right place for such an item.'

The transaction took less than seven minutes. Ida was just the correct cocktail of informed and polite, to make a quick sale, as she had been tutored by five of the best saleswomen in the City of Birmingham!

47

At the end of her second month, Ida was serving on a daily basis, but a form of shop floor hierarchy was observed, in that many of the ladies had their favourite assistant. Mrs Bingham, the rather curt wife of the most renowned lawyer in the city, would only be attended to by Martha. The other girls were only too happy for anyone but them to serve the occasionally obnoxious Mrs B. who Ida observed, appeared to have some similar traits to the despotic Rose!

One lunchtime, Eunice asked Ida to go upstairs and see her mother. Marjorie put down her accounts ledger and looking piercingly at Ida said, 'Ida, please get out of the room, come back in, walk up and down the salon four times and then sit down opposite me.'

Ida did as she was bid, head held high with hips forward, then settled herself in a high-backed armchair opposite her employer.

'Good, good, so much better, now do show me your hands and give me your best "knock them dead" smile.'

This accomplished, Ida sat expectantly.

'What do you know of sex, Ida? Please answer me honestly now.'

Ida felt herself getting warm in the dark green two-piece Eunice had gifted her; after looking at the top of Marjorie's head for a second or two, she answered slowly, 'Well, I know what goes where, what bits do what and all that Mrs Peyton.'

'And you, have you experienced sexual intercourse?'

'Well, I have done it a few times with my friend Wilma's brother Tommy back home. Another boy, Jonjo, wanted to as well, but I strung him along for a lark.'

'All right Ida that's enough. I don't need chapter and verse. Suffice it to say you clearly know what is what, well done. Now, off you pop back downstairs to work. Please ask Eunice to come up here when she is free.'

When Eunice came up to see her mother, she enquired, 'All well, Mother? Did you want to talk about next month's window theme?'

'No, no, not at this moment. I have just had Ida up here, and by the way, she looked very good in your two-piece cast off. I have had the talk; she will be grand. If we give her one more month, then she will be more than ready to help out at a card evening. Oh, and do make sure that she is scrupulous about cleaning her teeth. She certainly has a winning smile!'

When Ida got back downstairs, she told Martha about Mrs P. asking her about the sex thing.

'Oh yes, we all have had that conversation with her. She likes to know that we can handle ourselves in all manner of circumstances. You did tell her that you are not a virgin?'

'Oh yes, I told her about Tommy, she said it was good that I knew "what is what".'

48

Vera was pleased for her new friend. She knew how much Ida had hated the sorting office. The pair swam once a fortnight. Vera, relishing her newfound water wings, loved hearing all about her friend's new position, the well-to-do Divine customers, and Ida was not the least bit interested in hearing about Mrs Lambert's hawk eyes!

Janice had invited Ida to a Sunday tea at her marital home. A small narrow terraced house on Coppard Street. As Ida sat down at the kitchen table with the newlyweds, she thought Janice wouldn't be quitting her job anytime soon; she would need the money to sort this drab old place out which was ill-equipped with exhausted old furniture. There was a slight air of unease as Janice dished up a plate of leathery-looking liver and burnt bacon with watery overcooked cabbage, by her own admission no semblance of a cook. Ida felt Desmond would rather she was not having tea with them and to be honest, looking at her plate, so did she!

So she kept her chitter-chatter about her new job to a minimum.

At the end of their rather depressing meal which finished with lumpy custard poured over grey-tinged fruit from a can, Desmond sat blowing smoke across the small square table,

Ida took this as her signal to leave, which she was more than happy to do. Janice followed her to the front door, 'You all right, girly? Paying your dues to Mrs Pritchard on time?'

'Yes, I'm grand honestly, I feel so lucky to have found this new job, it is a smashing place to work and look, Eunice gave me this lovely dress. Of course, I'm paying up on the dot in the rent book; I don't want to be out on my ear then I would have to come and live here with you and Desmond,' laughing as she finished her sentence.

Walking to get a bus after leaving Janice's, Ida thought about the sex conversation that she had experienced with Marjorie; she wasn't really sure what to make of it all. It didn't bother her in the least. Back home there was sex everywhere what with mares and stallions, ewes and rams it was all around them. The fact that Martha, Peggy, Dina, and Lucy had all had the same talk pleased her that she was now in the same category, whatever that was, as them.

49

The girls at Divine had been surprised to hear after a few weeks of Ida beginning her new job, that her mother had abandoned her and vanished when she was just a toddler. They were as accustomed to Fathers "doing a runner" as they were to learn that "so and so was up the duff", but a mother leaving a small child was all new to them. All four of them were surprised by how well-adjusted and level-headed Ida appeared to be. She had chatted to them about Sylvie very openly and seemingly without much emotion.

'Do you want to find her Ida?' Peggy had asked one day when they were in the stock room for gift wrapping mock-up gift boxes for the festive window display.

'Folk always asks me that, always women. Do you know Peggy, I don't really remember her. My aunt and granda are sure that she left of her own free will, maybe with a new fella, maybe not. If she had the mind to do that to me, why the hell should I want to know her? As for my father, who knows? My mother probably didn't know!'

'I can see that if you feel that way about her, why would you care about reuniting with her? Anyway, you have a new family here at Divine. Here, put a green ribbon on this one for me Ida.'

Eunice had learnt of Sylvie's Houdini bath time act when they had met for the second time at the swimming baths. She was also struck by how extraordinarily apathetic Ida was about her mother's disappearance. Neither of them mentioned it again.

Marjorie had been informed of this nugget in Ida's back story when Eunice had first mentioned meeting her during her weekend swim. Prompting her mother to respond sharply, 'Well, that past circumstance will more than likely serve us well in the future, all assuming that she is a grafter and can sell.'

Ida's fashion knowledge blossomed along with her customer skills. When Lucy and Martha went down with a very nasty flu, she stepped up and had Mrs Danebury leave the showroom with not one but two beaded evening gowns and all the accessories. Garnering great plaudits from Eunice.

50

Janice found little time to see Ida, which suited Ida extremely well. Although she had always looked upon her mother's friend as a much older sister, she didn't fancy Janice knowing her every move. Feeling a great sense of wanting to "plough her own furrow" now that she had made it out of Marshcombe.

One early evening on the tram back to her digs, it occurred to her that she hadn't thought about Marshcombe for some time, so immersed was she in her new city life. She could not have imagined on leaving school, that she might have found herself working in such a high-end store so soon after arriving in Birmingham.

Never short on work ethic thanks to Maude and Elmer, Ida's own diligence, however, only extended to work that she enjoyed and working at Divine was one job she most certainly relished.

Once in a while, she wondered vaguely what Jonjo was up to and whether had he begun to ride in races or even had a winner.

Eunice had talked of a trip to the racecourse to thank the girls for their enthusiastic selling. *Perhaps,* she thought, *she might see him there and speculated whether he would seem more attractive to her out of the countryside and sporting colourful jockey's silks.*

51

In early March, on a relatively quiet day, Ida was helping Eunice conjure up a wonderful Easter-themed window, complete with seven black and white taxidermy rabbits, fresh carrots and enticing worsted and Barleycorn coloured coats and jackets elegantly displayed on wooden mannequins. Eunice passing Ida a heavy wooden box of recently delivered carrots said, 'Right, Ida, I would like you to help at this evening's soirée beginning at six o'clock. I will find you a suitable dress and shoes. Prepare to have your eyes opened and do please remember that we, here at Divine, do pride ourselves on our discretion. Some of our guests are prominent men in the city. When you are addressing them look them in the eye and do remember to smile, please.'

'Thank you, Eunice. I will not let you or Mrs Peyton down you will see.'

'Excellent, Ida, take your lead from the other girls and be mindful do not chatter too much and what happens in the salon stays in the salon. Good girl.'

The egg sandwich sat half nibbled on the plate in front of her. Ida's normally fearsome appetite had temporarily left her. She tried not to overthink the forthcoming evening, it was not the serving of drinks that concerned her, it was the worry that she might talk too much which stemmed from her exuberant confidence and excitement.

After chatting to Martha and Dina, her concerns lessened. Dina had said talking was fine as long as the gentlemen were not in play. If you took them a drink on the Venetian lace doily covered tray, place the glass down to the right of the guest and only speak if you are spoken to.

By 5:30, Ida was brimming with youthful excitement, eager to take a great gulp of this grown-up after-dark world.

Eunice had found a flattering burgundy red, cinched waisted mid-length dress, matched with half Louis heel patent leather shoes for her. Immediately Ida felt thoroughly adult. Never did she see anything as swanky as this in Mrs Noble's workshop. She also loved saying the word "swanky", something she had heard Peggy often say.

When Ida was ready in her new evening outfit, Eunice asked her to pop into the salon to do a "walk up" for her mother.

'Splendid, Ida, you gussy up extremely well. Now tell me what you have learnt about this evening?'

'Well, Mrs Peyton, I am to serve drinks but on no account make them. I must smile a lot and most of all don't chatter away like a rattling sewing machine. Oh, and take the gentlemen's coats and hang them up tidily.'

'Perfect. I knew you would be a quick learner. Now walk up and down the salon a few times and let me have a good look at you.'

Ida did as she was bid; she so enjoyed all this parading. It was a bit like showing off, which was actively discouraged back in Marshcombe. As she left the salon to return to the kitchen where the other girls were gathered, Marjorie was sporting a crimson-lipped grin.

52

At just after six o'clock, the first three guests arrived by the side door. A loud clanking sound of the big door knocker halted the girls in their final preening moments. Swiftly Martha went down the stairs and opened the door with an enthusiastic flourish.

'Good evening, gentlemen. Lovely evening for a game of cards. Do come on up.'

'Good evening to you, Martha,' they replied in a unison baritone chorus.

Once they reached the vestibule on the landing, Martha opened the door to the salon, where Eunice and Marjorie stood shiny and resplendent in dresses freshly off hangers from the clothing rails downstairs.

'Welcome, welcome, Major Delaney, Stanley, and Bernard. Please let the girls take your overcoats and get you some drinks.'

Lucy and Ida entered the salon which had been decorated with large crystal-cut glass vases brimming with the fresh bouquets of highly scented yellow roses that had been delivered by Donald earlier that day.

'Now, Major Delaney, may I introduce you to our newest assistant Ida; she has not long been with us, all the way from

South Warwickshire.' Ida, hearing her prompt, as per her earlier instructions, stepped towards the very upright blue-suited Major, and thrust forward her right hand.

'Good evening, Major Delaney. I am Ida. May I take your coat for you?'

Relieved to have remembered to look the not unhandsome Major in the eye, she took his Astrakan collared coat from him and hung it on the coat stand in the vestibule. As Ida briefly left the room, the Major, or Thomas, to his friends shot Marjorie a lugubrious wink and a steady smile.

Ida returned to repeat the procedure with Stanley Simcox who owned several jewellers and clock shops in the Midlands. Finally introducing herself to Bernard Lewis, Lucy had just told her that he was a quantity surveyor, which meant absolutely nothing to her!

It struck Ida as she hung up Mr Lewis's heavy tweed coat, that these three men seemed ancient, although none of them were over forty-six and that they seemed delighted to be there in Marjorie's decorous salon.

Dina organised the drinks, and Ida delivered the Major's whisky and soda on a tray; with not a drop split and her award-winning smile.

Some twenty minutes later, Dennis King hammered the knocker ferociously and Ida was dispatched downstairs to greet him.

'Well, hello, my dear! Haven't seen you here before.'

'Good evening, sir. I am Ida, the new girl.'

'Well, Ida, it is a pleasure to meet you, lead me to a stiff drink, please. I have had the devil of a day in court.'

He followed Ida up the stairs despite her gesturing to him to go first.

Ida began to think that this overtime was a right lark. His Honour Judge King was swiftly followed by the arrival of an enormously tall man, Alistair Ettingham-Forbes owner of a beautiful estate out near Coleshill and Philip Sully the mildly eccentric artist.

Once they had exchanged various male pleasantries and kissed Marjorie on each cheek, the men settled down at the card tables, Marjorie playing with the judge, Philip Scully and Bernard Lewis. The other four men made up the second table. They warmed up with a game of Belote with no cash involved.

The girls retreated to the kitchen, not before sneaking a bottle of gin out with them. Eunice tended to remain hovering in the salon, plumping cushions and generally attentive to the games.

Peggy asked Ida if she drank alcohol.

'Oh yes, cider is my favourite, I used to drink it with my friend Jonjo, you know the boy from the racing stable who wanted to do me,' she offered laughing.

'Well, look, Ida, gin is much, much stronger, so just have a small sip from my glass.'

Ida took something resembling a gulp and immediately regretted it pulling an "I'm not doing that again" face. Peggy and Dina laughed whilst Lucy and Martha rolled their eyes theatrically.

About half an hour later, Eunice came into the kitchen, 'Martha and Dina, please go and top up the drinks. Ida, you may go home. You have done very well for your first evening. See you tomorrow.'

As Ida put on her coat, a rich chocolate brown one, that Eunice had procured for her; she could still feel the gin catching in the back of her throat. *Ugh*, she thought that was vile. However, the evening hadn't been such hard work after all, and the guests were so well-dressed and polite.

The following morning, as Eunice and Marjorie were readying themselves to leave the house, Eunice asked her mother how she thought Ida had done the previous evening.

'She was a natural, very engaging and followed her instructions beautifully.' And then, after dispensing a couple of pats to the indulged Pico, they left for Divine.

53

That weekend Ida met Janice for a cup of tea and an iced bun. Janice was keen to hear all about Ida's job, without the constriction of Desmond's presence.

'Janice,' said Ida enthusiastically, 'the clothes are beautiful, so well made, Mrs Noble and Maude would faint if they saw them. All the other girls are very friendly and the employer's daughter Eunice has helped me with so much.'

'Well, I can see that they are putting some fancy manners on you! Just make sure you write to Maudie and pay your rent on time.'

It was clear to Ida that Janice had short-changed herself in her marriage to Desmond, not a man ever possessed of a riveting personality, but once they were hitched any semblance of one deserted him. Janice, although not as spirited as the effervescent Sylvie, was fun and interested in life, but found sitting across the kitchen table opposite her husband whilst he scrutinised the *Birmingham Post* every evening a dispiriting chore. She often thought of what her friend might be doing, of one thing she was sure of; she would definitely not be sitting opposite a Desmond and cooking offal which he delighted in scoffing in a noisy fashion!

Janice was glad that Ida did not mention her mother. *After all the years that had passed, it was for the best,* she always thought.

Ida had blossomed into a striking-looking girl; she walked with a combination of her well-held previous athleticism and her newly acquired Divine refinement. Her country enthusiasm for cycling most, by necessity, and her penchant for swimming had gifted her an enviably toned body. Certainly, she was aware of men artfully taking a double glance as she strode along the pavement. This male behaviour amused her and instilled in her a deep-rooted feeling that men were easily manipulated; not in the vile bullying manner of Rose but in a more subtle sense.

Ida was delighted to see an extra two shillings in her wage packet at the end of the week after her first soirée. Keen to continue with this upturn in her finances, Ida asked Eunice when she might be needed again and was happy to learn that the following Thursday she would be required.

'Ida, you were an asset to us last time you helped, and I knew you would be. Our Major Delaney was delighted to meet you, quite a hit you were. Make sure you wear the cream and caramel dress I gave you a few weeks ago.'

The following Thursday, as Ida entered the kitchen to make a lunchtime pot of tea for them all, Peggy was remarking, 'Has anyone else noticed Ida's funny left ear?'

'My mother bit the top bit of my left ear when I was a baby because I wouldn't stop crying,' Ida said.

'Oh, Ida, that is awful, poor you. It must have been so painful.'

Ida laughing so hard that she was sounding like a braying donkey replied, 'Ha ha, no, she didn't, just joking with you. I was born with this raggedy edge to the top of my left ear.'

'You had us all going there Ida, come on get that brew on and make it good and strong we have a busy afternoon and evening.'

'Who is playing this evening, does anyone know?' asked Lucy.

Martha, through sips of piping hot sweet tea offered, 'The Milkman is in I think and Spatchcock.'

'I didn't know the milkman was invited to card games.'

'No, no, Ida not our milkman. The Milkman is our nickname for Major Delaney and Spatchcock is Bernard Lewis.'

'Why do you call them that?'

All four of the other girls fell about laughing with Dina laughing and wheezing at the same time due to a hard case of a Capstan cigarette habit. Eventually, Peggy said, 'Oh, Ida you will find out soon enough!'

Marjorie had been in a foul frame of mind all day. No amount of carefully presented pots of tea had restored her equilibrium. Normally on a card night, she was very cheerful. But Philip Scully owed her eleven pounds, and she was beginning to wonder whether she would ever see it. Then to make matters worse, on returning from a civilised lunch with dear Donald at Morton's, she came upon Roland skulking in the side passage clearly a great deal the worse for wear from cheap beer, judging by the stink of him. Marjorie, with a piercing voice, called out, 'Roland what on earth do you think you are doing?' as he was about to unbutton his trousers fly and urinate up against the smart blue side door.

'Er Mrs P, how are you going? Er...I was just...' he trailed as he registered the steam of Marjorie's anger and pent-up frustration coming at him like a burst factory boiler.

'Get yourself off my property at once and do me a favour, stay away you nitwit.'

'Ah, I only want to see your lovely Eunice and play cards with all them fancy gentlemen.'

One of the girls had forgotten a metal bucket after washing the door that morning. Marjorie put down her black leather handbag, picked up the bucket and, with one careful swing, threw the contents over Roland's head.

'Do I make myself clear?'

There was no response from Roland as he staggered aqueously towards the road. Marjorie stomped into the showroom demanding to know who had left the bucket there. In hindsight, Lucy's forgetfulness had come in very handy!

54

The drinks cabinet was plentifully re-stocked, minus the gin bottle that the girls had craftily swiped previously. Ida, stunning in the caramel and cream dress, looked most attractive as she stood ready at the bottom of the stairs like an eager sentry on guard.

In the flurry of readiness, she had forgotten to ask why a delivery of forty pints of gold top milk had been made that day. One thing she knew for sure was that neither Mrs P nor Eunice would be making milk puddings for their guests. Only alcohol was ever served.

First to arrive, somewhat early, was Philip Sully who greeted Ida cheerily and accompanied her upstairs to the salon sporting an eye-catching maroon velvet jacket and black silk scarf. As Ida was heading back downstairs to her meet-and-greet position, she overheard Marjorie saying, 'Well, thank you, Philip, for paying your dues, so good that this is all cleared up, come let Dina get you a drink.'

The other gentlemen arrived at staggered intervals, all appearing most congenial and quite possibly having already had a few "sherbets" on board. That evening there were only six visitors to the salon.

Eunice had asked Ida that morning to help Lucy with any tasks that might need two pairs of hands. Of course, Ida had replied that she would be more than happy to assist Lucy, who Ida had grown to like very much since she started work at Divine.

The six men sat down to a game of poker. Marjorie unusually was a mere onlooker but never missing a trick, whilst making very discreet pencil notes in a tiny calf-skin-covered journal that she had bought in London in Burlington Arcade some months before.

An hour or so later and many more drinks consumed, the men finished the game. Leaving the card table, they settled themselves on the elegant and very comfortable chairs and couches.

The girls, having congregated in the kitchen, were snapped to attention by Eunice appearing in the doorway and clicking her fingers in the air above her head. Obligingly the girls trooped into the salon where yet more drinks were topped up.

Lucy then went to sit next to Major Delaney on one of the couches and Peggy sat laughing with Stanley Simcox. Martha was listening to Judge King being wonderfully erudite and indiscreet about a case he had recently heard in the Crown court. Finally, Dina was standing at the far end of the room in conversation with Alistair Ettingham-Forbes. Ida heard him say something about his father-in-law dying. *Well, that is cheerful,* she thought, as she observed Dina nodding sympathetically. Philip Sully was talking to Eunice.

Some ten minutes later Eunice asked Ida to come to the kitchen.

'Ida, it is time for you to shine. Please take the milk crates that were delivered this morning to the bathroom.'

'Oh yes, what right now?'

'Yes, straight away.' Ida did as she was bid, taken aback at how heavy the bottles and wooden crates were.

On completion of this bizarre request, Ida went back into the salon where the chatting continued unabated. Lucy and the Major then stood up, with Lucy beckoning Ida to follow her. This she did and to her utter astonishment was led into the bathroom. Whereupon the Major sat down on a chair and loosened his tie. Ida thought it best to focus on Lucy after all she was there to help her.

'Please help me empty the milk into the bath Ida.' Nodding in response, the two girls emptied all the milk into the bath, with Lucy shooting Ida a reassuring wink.

Lucy then asked Ida to run the bath to a nice warm temperature, whilst she undressed and put on a black silk robe that hung on the back of the door.

Ida knelt conscientiously by the bath stirring the water to the correct temperature with her back to Major Delaney who was by now down to his underwear and still sporting his sock garters! The bath ready, Lucy rehung the robe and strode purposefully towards the bath before gracefully stepping into it and lowering herself into the creamy water whilst telling Ida to stand by the door.

Like Cleopatra herself, Lucy lay in the milky bath with her peachy breasts partially submerged, whilst the Major sat fixated as this erotic scene unfolded. It was all Ida could do not to erupt into hysterical laughter as she watched this scene unfold. She clamped her jaw shut in a vice-like manner hoping to stem the laughter that was brewing inside of her.

The Major now completely naked, stood up and looking at Lucy said, 'May I wash you?'

'But Major of course you can.'

At the same time, her hand came out of the warm water, and as she looked at him, fluttering her eyelashes, she said, 'Please do use this lovely soft natural sponge.'

The Major knelt down beside the cast iron roll top bath and began gently and caressingly to wash Lucy in the opaque bath water. Whilst the object of his desire lay back and shut her eyes. Then as Lucy's left hand rose out of the water reaching for the Major's tumescent pleasure sword, she said with eyes still closed, 'Ida, you may leave us now.'

Once out on the landing, Ida could no longer contain her laughter and thought it best to go downstairs to prevent anyone from hearing her, put her face into the crook of her elbow and then once alone released it like the air from a balloon. It took many minutes before she could stem her laughter. Once downstairs she thought the whole bathroom scene was one of the funniest things she had ever seen. It took many minutes before she could regain her composure.

On returning to the salon, she discovered that Martha and Judge King and Peggy and Stanley Simcox were not there. Only Alistair Ettingham-Forbes and Dina remained in deep conversation. *Bet he is still harping on about dying people*, Ida thought.

Meanwhile, in the kitchen, Marjorie and Eunice sat at the table counting a considerable amount of cash.

'Ah, there you are, Ida. Would you please collect the glasses from the salon and then wash and dry them.'

'Eunice, may I ask you something?' said Ida.

'Let us talk tomorrow, Ida, I will be in late, but we will have a chat. When you have done the glasses, you may go home.'

Ida had a good grasp of what was going on at the soirées. An observant girl and crafty with it, she had eavesdropped on many a private conversation between Eunice and her mother.

She was surprised that the girls had not said more to her about the "extra" entertainment. But perhaps they had been told by Marjorie to keep quiet so as not to send her scooting back to the countryside; no chance of that thought Ida drowsily as she fell asleep.

Up early the following morning, energised by the prospect of the talk with Eunice, Ida did forty-five lengths at the baths on her way into Divine. She hoped that when she saw Lucy, she wouldn't start giggling.

She found the girls drinking tea in the kitchen before opening the store.

'Want a tea, Ida?' asked Dina manning the pot.

'Yes, thanks, two sugars, please. I've just been swimming. Lucy, did you have a nice bath?'

The five girls began to giggle until they were all laughing infectiously.

'Well done, Ida, you did good, we knew you would be dandy with the "horizontal" refreshment menu.' Martha offered and more laughter ensued.

Just after Ida's lunch break, Eunice called her into the salon. Marjorie was out lunching with Donald.

'Sit down, Ida. You are a bright girl, and I fully expect by now that you have a pretty good idea of what we supply here at Divine and refer to as some extra "French polishing" services. Some of these men have unhappy home lives, and we try to bring them some cheer now and again. Next Thursday I would like you to assist Dina on card night.'

Ida hesitated, needing a few seconds to gauge her response.

'I'm okay with all of that. I used to hear from the jockeys that they sometimes visited a place in Droitwich. Mind you, don't think they were unhappy, just horny! How much extra money would I be able to earn Eunice?'

'Well, once you have moved onto entertaining one of the gentlemen and "rump scuttle" is on the menu, then it will be a guinea. Our gentlemen do have some diverse requests such as you saw last night.'

'Can I say no to a request that I don't like?'

'Yes, of course, Ida. Now pop back down to the showroom and send Lucy up to me.'

55

Eunice had felt a gratifying sense of being right in trusting her instincts when she had come across Ida that morning at the swim baths. She was stunned to have overheard on at least two occasions Marjorie praising Ida for her newfound manners or some such improvements. Praise and compliments had never been very forthcoming in Eunice's direction. She felt that her mother believed that a modicum of encouragement would go a very long way and that too much appreciation would make her daughter soft.

With no memory of her father, she had wondered many times how very different their lives might have been, had he not been struck down so helpfully by that tram. Her mother never talked about him, there were no pictures and certainly no keepsakes of him in the house. She admired her mother in many respects watching her build two successful businesses from scratch. But she was also quite aware of just how difficult she could be. It was more than the typical mother/daughter relationship clash. Once Eunice, as a twelve-year-old, had begun shadowing her mother at work and witnessed her interaction with other people other than Dorothy, she became only too aware of her mother's utter lack of empathy for others.

It had always struck her how odd it was that she had befriended dear Donald. Perhaps he saw something in Marjorie that she did not.

One of the things Eunice found so confoundingly irritating about her mother was her complete lack of interest in a conversation unless it concerned business. She did, however, display a masterclass in feigned interest in what the other person was saying. Although the pair of them did share a common trait in avarice, no doubt this had been infused in plentiful supply via Marjorie's placenta.

Eunice had never questioned the fact that her mother ran a somewhat uniquely bespoke business after shop hours. To her, as a child, it represented fine treats and fancy clothes, and when Marjorie was busy in the evenings, she had the stable and dependable Dorothy to play board games with whilst drinking hot chocolate.

When Eunice turned fifteen, Marjorie gave her a tattered fabric-covered book of elaborate ink drawings illustrating graphic and varied sexual positions. At the bottom of each drawing, there was a caption in Chinese symbols. The book itself was not such a surprise but the Chinese symbols were something unexpected. Marjorie told her to have a good look through the book and on no account to let Dorothy see it. Study them she did and judging by the state of the pages, a great many people had also thumbed their way through it before it had found its way into Marjorie's hands!

A few days later Marjorie sat on her daughter's bed and asked, 'Did you understand the positions?'

Even for her mother, Eunice had felt that this was an interesting approach to the "birds and the bees" conversation.

'Yes, mother, I did. I have seen a French book that Emmie showed me in the toilets at school. It was similar, but your Chinese one is a lot more advanced you might say.'

'I came across the book in a small bookseller in King's Cross. The drawings are so well-executed. Now, not all but some of those bodily contortions are requested by my gentlemen. Most of them are relatively conservative in terms of positions, but it is best to be prepared.'

'Well, I touched my toes this morning before getting dressed.' Eunice ventured, stabbing vaguely at being humorous.

'Right my girl, it is worth remembering that throughout your life try to focus on being as womanly as possible. If done well, it can be very potent.'

'Am I to start work upstairs, Mother?'

'There is my girl, a premium on your chastity. I have two very agreeable men who would be prepared to pay a very special dividend to have the honour of taking your cherry. I am just in the process of fine-tuning the negotiations to see who has the winning bid.'

'When will this take place, Mother?'

'Oh, soon enough, Eunice, come on let us walk to Oxedene Park and buy ice creams.'

Three weeks later, Edward Faulkner, a thirty-something pudgy-faced solicitor had secured the winning ticket, at a healthy one hundred guineas. The somewhat speedy deed took place on a Sunday afternoon in the back bedroom above Divine's showroom. Eunice was compliant and had no need to be youthfully supple! Edward was both courteous and efficient. All Eunice had thought was that Edward Faulkner needed a new razor as she lay beneath him observing the patches of stubble on his chin and upper lip.

And so, Eunice was indoctrinated.

56

Ida had placated and stalled for as long as she could. Maude's letters had become more and more imploring as each one was placed in the communal letter box in Mrs Pritchard's hallway. It seemed a visit to Marshcombe was unavoidable if she was to stem the anxious flow of worry that Maude displayed in her missives. More importantly, she could not run the risk, although an unlikely one at that, of Maude finding the wherewithal to visit Birmingham.

Nervous about asking for time off, as she worked every Saturday, Ida timed her request perfectly, catching Marjorie as she returned from a clearly mostly liquid lunch with Donald at the Forum Hotel. Marjorie told her that of course, she should visit her aunt and that she could have the following Saturday off but to be sure to be back in the showroom by midday on the Monday. Eunice was slightly taken aback by Marjorie's unaccustomed forbearance.

As Ida sat on the bus heading towards Marshcombe in Eunice's cast-off dark green jacket and skirt, she wondered if Maude and her granda would see a great difference in her.

At last, the bus came to a loud belching stop in Marshcombe, and she saw Maudie and Elmer waving animatedly. After hugs all around and much making of how "all grown-up and fancy" she looked, the trio headed to the cottage for some of Maude's delicious hot oven-baked ham with parsley sauce and mashed potato for lunch. She had really wanted to push the boat out for her niece's first visit back home.

'How is the new job working out, Ida?' Elmer ventured as he dolloped more sauce onto his plate.

'Oh, I love it! There are four other girls and the boss's daughter who works there also. Maudie, you would love the clothes, so fine and fancy. Eunice gave me this suit smart, isn't it?'

'Yes, it's lovely on you. You look well and happy, and they treat you right?'

'Oh yes, they are very good employers. Think I will find my old bicycle and go to see Granda later.'

Maude was almost transfixed by the dramatic change in her niece and said quietly, 'He would be so happy to see you. Your old bike is down the side of the wood store. Be sure to be back for supper. I'm doing us all a treat and roasting a chicken with all the trimmings.'

Happy to be reunited with her tired old bicycle, she pondered whether to take it back to Birmingham with her. It would save on tram and bus fares.

As she swooped into the farmyard, she found her grandfather standing at the top of the suspiciously fragile-looking wood steps which led up to the hay loft.

'Hello, Granda!' she bellowed.

James could not get down the ladder quickly enough to greet his granddaughter.

'Hello, my girl. Well, look at you, all dandy. How is the big city treating you then?'

The two of them spent a happy hour and a half chatting contentedly and drinking big milky mugs of tea. Ida was delighted by the fact that Rose was resting with a bad headache. James had sad news to impart. Kipper had suddenly and fatally collapsed after leaving the cottage of a Mrs Nora Faulkner, in the village of Puddstone. Falling forward as his heart failed; his fall was broken by the large Victoria sponge and a ginger cake that he was carrying.

Ida was sad to hear this as she had been well aware that he had kept an eye out for her as she grew up. She wondered what Mr Faulkner had said on hearing the news! Then, before she set off for the cottage in Dingley, she asked to see the horses. James brimmed with pride as they looked at them grazing peacefully in the top field. Leaning on top of the old wooden gate he quietly said, 'Oh, if only our Sylvie could see her now.'

Ida wasn't sure if he was thinking out loud as the statement was not much more than a whisper.

The following morning, Sunday, she cycled up to Durent's. As she opened the main yard gate, she heard a long loud wolf whistle. To her left she saw Pecker laughing and grinning so hard that the corners of his mouth almost touched his ears.

'Jonjo is going to be gutted, Ida.'

'Why is that, Pecker, you moron?'

''Cos he is working up in Malton, Yorkshire now, left last month.'

'He told me he wanted to be a jockey. Is his dad still here?'

'He has been promised rides by his new trainer. Yes, Paul is still based here. Fancy a drink with me later?'

As she athletically swung her right leg over her bike, she said, 'Nice try, Pecker! You are old enough to be my dad. See ya.'

As soon as the words left her voice box, she regretted it. Pecker retorted loudly, 'Ha ha ha ha, but you don't know who he is.'

As the 8:15 Monday morning bus bound for Birmingham drew away from Marshcombe, Ida sat looking out of the window and realised that her visit had only confirmed what she already knew, she did not belong in Dingley nor Marshcombe. Next to her was a basket of Maude's wholesome homemade fayre, which was sure to sustain her for a few days.

57

Ida's visit back to the countryside and seeing her family again had been a real eye-opener and totally reaffirmed her convictions that Birmingham was the only place for her. This awakening was like being given a sudden injection of euphoria for her new and exciting life!

When she reached the showroom, all four girls were surreptitiously eating fancy embossed chocolates that sat enticingly in a silver box under the counter, a gift apparently from a grateful Philip Sully. Peggy, noisily sucking the strawberry-flavoured fondant out of one of the chocolates said, 'Here, Ida, try the ones with the walnuts on top. How did it go, your weekend in the fields?'

'I had a great time thanks, Peg. Think that will keep my aunt off my back for a while. Have we got a busy week?'

'Yes, we have a full house on Wednesday, and you will be helping me. Sidney Simcox will be our special project. If that doesn't open your eyes wide and test your poor skills at holding in the laughter, I don't know what will! Come on girls let's finish these before Mrs P or Eunice catches us.'

Sidney Simcox, a neat pixie of a man with horn-rimmed glasses had won the early evening poker game and was in high spirits. But that might also have had much to do with his enjoying three of Dina's potent "Trouser Trampler" cocktails. It was a given that the merrier the gentlemen were then potentially the bigger the tips!

Sidney asked Peggy if they might find somewhere a little quieter. So, Peggy, Sidney, and Ida retreated to the middle bedroom. This was not an over large room but decorated in green-grey colours and furnished simply with a double bed, four comfortable-looking chairs and a washstand with towels on the underside rail. A large, framed mirror hung on the wall at the end of the bed.

Sidney was carrying a large black leather holdall which he placed on the chair by the door. Addressing Ida he said, 'Be a good girl and give me a hand will you.'

Peggy mouthed to Ida that she was going to the bathroom to "prepare". Meanwhile, Sydney had removed his suit jacket hanging it on the hook on the back of the door. He then unfastened the bag and, to Ida's total amazement, pulled out of it a white rabbit fur suit, complete with a pert wire rabbit fur-eared hood. Ida, who by this time had stalk-like eyes, was astounded; *I don't believe this,* she thought to herself.

'How can I help you Mr Simcox?' she said.

'Ida, I need you to fasten me at the back once I get into my rabbit and help me with the hood.'

By now, Sidney Simcox was standing before her stark naked in advance of climbing nimbly into the bunny outfit complete with fluffy brown bob tail.

Peggy had returned and sat on the bed in a pink flowered robe observing Ida fastening "her gentleman" into his transformation from jeweller to a White Beveren Rabbit. Sidney then produced a small brown bag of washed carrots which he gave to Peggy. He was now covered from head to ankles in fur which although Ida thought was so lovely and soft could not help but think how hot he would get!

His bare feet seemed at odds with this metamorphosis into his world of fantasy. The suit had an opening at the crutch from which his pink flute protruded. The "rabbit" then reached into the pocket of his trousers, which were neatly folded over the back of the chair and handed Ida twenty-five shillings. Pressing it into her hand, he said, 'Thank you my dear, Peggy and I will be alone now.'

58

Five days a week the salon, bedrooms, kitchen, and bathroom were scrupulously cleaned by Irish Ivy. A tiny, not overclever young girl with a round melon-like face who almost always wore a permanently perplexed expression. Although she had had enough wits about her to have knocked on Divine's side door looking for work and by the shambles of her a good hot meal too.

Eunice had asked her inside to meet Marjorie. Once they had completed their probing questions as to her experience, with Marjorie attempting to appear the benevolent future employer, the two Divine women had deduced that Irish Ivy would be a good fit as a cleaner for them. Given the fact that she had left County Kilkenny in Ireland after a great deal of difficult "family bother" and that she knew no one in Birmingham, she would be eternally grateful for the work. But best of all, as far as the Peyton women were concerned, Ivy did not possess an enquiring mind.

One of the girls would let her in by the blue side door and then she would disappear up the narrow stairs to scrub and polish to her heart's content. As she did her work, Ivy could be heard humming some sort of Irish folk song whilst she set the fire grates ready for lighting. She also enjoyed the heady scent of the fresh lilies as she dusted around the big glass vases sometimes standing still and cupping them with her hands inhaling long and hard.

From the first month of Ivy beginning work, Eunice had subtly pencil-marked the bottles of alcohol and decanters. Not a drop went astray during her zealous cleaning forays in the salon.

One day when she was washing the bathroom floor, she spotted a black sock garter under the chair. Not even this sparked an iota of curiosity in her bird-witted brain nor even removing the empty milk bottles in their crates! Picking it up she simply looped it over a hook on the back of the bathroom door and merrily continued her back-and-forth scrubbing motion.

"Irish" as Peggy had named her, never entered the showroom and scuttled out of sight if one of the girls went upstairs. Once she had completed her tasks speaking to nobody, she left Divine. It meant that Dina, Martha, Lucy, and Peggy were only too pleased not to have to do any more charring chores themselves.

Meanwhile, Philip Sully hoped to redeem himself in Marjorie's eyes after his tardiness in paying his gambling debts. He had been commissioned to paint the portrait of a middle-ranking aristocrat's wife for a handsome fee. However, despite depicting the lady concerned as a beautiful fine-featured woman of elegant proportions, none of these bore any resemblance to the sitter! The aristocrat and his good lady wife were extremely delighted with the finished oil painting and gave Philip a generous "thank you" on top of his agreed fee.

This stroke of good fortune bought him some time to find his next commission. So, Philip decided to use his studio hours to paint Marjorie four erotic pieces to hang in the salon or bedrooms. One depicting fellatio, one a scene of mildly sensual bondage involving ribbons and another of a young man "riding below the crupper". The final painting was of two women, one gloriously Rubenesque the other lean and taught kissing each other passionately.

Both Marjorie and Eunice were captivated by the gifts and eagerly asked Donald to help them with the safe hanging of the paintings in the largest of the four bedrooms. Immediately sparking the idea in Marjorie that this bedroom should command a higher fee when used by one of the gentlemen.

Philip Sully had a penchant for Martha. He was forty-one, had a firm commitment phobia and enjoyed the better things in life but so very rarely could afford them. He rented a small house in Kings Heath but originated from Kent, telling Martha at their first "jump up" that he couldn't recall how he had landed up in Birmingham.

Of all the guests, Philip Sully was the most straightforward in the horizontal refreshment department. He liked to lie on the bed next to Martha, both naked and sharing a Lucky Strike cigarette. Although long gone were the days when it was rumoured that a Lucky Strike might contain marijuana, Philip Sully lived in hope!

The sex was perfunctory and energetic; once the deed was done the pair shared another "Strike" dressed and left the bedroom. The girls referred to Philip as "an easy" meaning very little effort was required on their part. It had been drummed into them from the very start that if they happened across one of the guests outside of Divine, they were to treat them as strangers.

It had amused Martha to ponder what the outcome might have been if one of them had been up in court before Judge King. Whether and how he might have influenced the jury!

59

On a grey October day, Ida turned seventeen. As she entered the upstairs kitchen where the girls, including Eunice, were congregated they clamoured, 'Happy birthday, Ida,' in a happy chorus.

The birthday girl was slightly taken aback by their jollity and particularly by the sight of a very fancy-looking chocolate birthday cake garnished with Maraschino cherries which sat magnificently on the kitchen table. As Eunice presented the cake to her, Ida said, 'Thank you. This looks so good. Do we have time for it before opening, Eunice?'

'Oh, I think so Ida, go ahead get the cake slicer and let us all have some.'

By opening time at ten o'clock, almost three-quarters of the cake had been consumed by the girls. Before heading downstairs to the salon, Eunice said, 'Ida, just a quick word in your shell-like ear. How would you feel about kissing and perhaps a touch more with Lucy?'

Ida finished drying the cake slicer and said, 'Well, I never thought about getting Buskey with a girl before.'

'Getting Buskey, what do you mean?'

'Getting Buskey is what we call kissing and petting in the countryside.'

'Oh yes, one of your entertaining quaintly rustic yokel phrases. Well, what do you say?'

Thinking for a moment Ida replied, 'Okay, I could give it a try maybe if I didn't like it, I could pretend? Is this for one of the gentlemen?'

'Yes, Ida it is, and pretending would be just fine. Judge King has a particular "bent" in that he does rather relish a "three's up". That would be himself and two of you girls.'

'This would help me make a good extra money I'm guessing.'

'Yes, of course, and it is your first experience of full involvement with one of our gentlemen. This I would make very clear to the judge; he will pay handsomely no doubt about that!'

After work that day, the girls gathered in the Red Lion to properly celebrate Ida's birthday, and as they drank their glasses of port, she asked Lucy, 'Eunice told me we are to have a "three's up" with the old judge, and I am to get "it on" with you. Will you help me along Lucy, please? Show me the ropes.'

'Ida honestly you just "mirror" my actions and it will be dandy. The judge is like a two-stroke pump, it will be over before we have smudged our lipsticks.'

This reaped a cacophony of girlish cackling, so much so the other drinkers turned to look at the girls' table.

Peggy said, 'Drink up you lot let's get off to our homes. We need to be fresh and sparkling for soirée night tomorrow.'

'What? Don't you mean we need to be ready for "line our pockets night",' Dina quipped.

The following night Marjorie was playing poker which prompted Sidney Simcox to say, 'Prepare to leave without a bean—Marjorie Peyton is at the tables.'

Marjorie, not one to enjoy any form of mickey taking if it involved her, chose to ignore this comment and concentrate on winning her hand. Thinking as she did so, that she would charge Sidney well over the odds next time he had the pleasure of using the big bedroom.

Dina did a roaring trade in cocktails making sure, as she always did, that she noted in the small pink ledger which of the gentlemen had ordered which liquid refreshments, being careful not to use the girls' nicknames for the clients in the ledger. Some of the men would have the privilege of monthly accounts but not Philip Sully or Ernest Hemple who was one of the largest landlords in the city. But had a reputation for being akin to a basking shark when it came to money.

Eunice had been surprised that her mother had sanctioned his participation in the soirées. But Ernest with his cut-throat sharp wit, expensive cologne and handmade shoes knew how to "blow hot air" in Marjorie's direction and had been granted a warm welcome.

It amused Eunice to observe her mother when a man was attempting to charm her. This rarely succeeded and was only ever successful to a small degree. Marjorie had never been the sort of woman to be swayed by a member of the opposite sex. But occasionally she did allow herself the odd mild toying if the mood took her, and Ernest Hemple very often arrived brandishing two bottles of the most deliciously expensive champagne. These bottles were snaffled away by Eunice into a locked cupboard in the kitchen, secure until opened for

Marjorie's private and personal consumption very often after she had summed up the night's takings.

Marjorie had never had the need to hustle for soirée business. Initially, she had mentioned to Donald that she was planning to start card evenings. He, with his very many connections, had earnestly spread the word. This resulted in a flurry of enthusiastic participants with word spreading like butter in a hot pan.

Marjorie and Eunice had been delighted with their latest protégé's progress. Eunice had been right to trust her finely tuned instincts inherited from her mother. She had seen pluck and poise in Ida, not just the boldness of teenage youth but something more; a sense of fearlessness and perhaps self-possession.

Mother and daughter had simultaneously agreed that Ida had come to hand swiftly enough and that she was well enough prepared to handle clients. They could not run the risk of a new girl giving a moderate service after all their hard endeavours in establishing an exceptional high-end and quality service, which had to be maintained at all times.

60

One evening soon after Ida's birthday, Judge King arrived at Divine in exuberantly good spirits. He had a week-long sabbatical from his wife Kathleen of twenty-four years, as she was visiting her aged unwell mother in Yorkshire. He declined a game of poker not wishing, despite being a canny player himself, to take on "the fiend" as he referred to Marjorie but never to her face.

Dina made him one of her new cocktails, which she had named in his honour, the "Menage à Trois". This was not so much a new creation but a vodka martini with a new name! But all the same, it had the designated effect of buffing the judge's ego. He was finishing off his fourth when he asked Ida and Lucy to join him in the green bedroom.

Lucy thought to herself, *He would fall asleep if he had another one.* Once in the bedroom he slumped onto the end of the bed, dropping his suit jacket and tie onto the floor behind him in a heap. Lucy took Ida by the hand and the two of them knelt at the head of the bed, facing one another. As Lucy unbuttoned Ida's pale grey dress, she ran her hands through Lucy's thick hair. Ida felt emboldened and kissed her neck gently, Lucy let out a purring sound. As the girls continued to undress one another, the judge stripped from the waist down leaving his shirt hanging down over his hairy buttocks.

Ida, despite concentrating on following her colleague's lead, afforded herself a sideways glance at the now puce-faced judge thinking bet he had kept his shirt on to hide his large expansive gut.

Once the girls were naked, they began ferociously to French kiss. The judge manoeuvred his way onto the bed between them. Oddly he hadn't uttered a word. The vodka and excitement seemingly rendered him mute. He heaved himself up onto his knees and pushed Lucy slightly further up the bed and onto her back. As he grappled his way on top of her, he let out a loud grunting sound, followed almost immediately by some very impressive snoring.

At this point, Ida was almost dressed and was quietly laughing as she helped Lucy extricate herself from under the comatose judge. As the pair finished dressing and adjusting their hair in the mirror, Lucy said quietly, 'You were spot on Ida, that will be a nice few extra quid for us. Come on let's pinch a drink and have a ciggy on the stairs.'

Ida followed Lucy out onto the landing where they found Marjorie hovering and looking at her watch.

'All well with our Judge King then girls?'

'Yes, all good, but he is now out for the count face down on the counterpane snoring,' Lucy replied. Ida was doing her level best not to laugh.

'Well, well, that is absolutely no good at all girls. I am running a whoring house not a boarding house. Make him a strong cup of tea and send him on his way. I must have a word with Dina about those Martinis.'

Turning on her heels she swished down the landing and back into the salon.

Once in the kitchen, Lucy began moaning about not being a bloody skivvy. Strong tea brewed and the two girls returned to the sleeping heap. Try as they might, they could not wake him. Even when they rolled him onto his back, which increased the volume of the snoring, he still slept. Ida went back to the kitchen and put some cold water into a small milk jug. Back in the bedroom, she began to flick little droplets of water onto the judge's forehead which began to trickle into his ears.

Suddenly and rather dramatically he sat bolt upright looking as though he didn't know where he was. Lucy said in her politest voice leaning towards him, 'Mrs Peyton thinks it would be best if you went home now.' Although given the state of Judge King if Lucy had barked at him like a rabid dog, he would not have noticed. The girls left him to get dressed having handed him the now less than hot tea.

Back in the kitchen Lucy and Ida finally had time for a cigarette and a few swigs from the judge's flask.

'Do they often fall asleep?' Ida asked.

'Sometimes the older ones tend to. Peggy says men are conditioned like that.'

'That was money for old rope. We weren't in the bedroom more than ten minutes,' Ida said.

'I told you he would be done in no time. How did you feel about getting Buskey with me?'

'It was no trouble, you tasted of ciggies and rum.'

They heard the green bedroom door open and slow footsteps on the landing then Marjorie's voice asking, 'Have you had a pleasant evening, Judge, with our new girl?'

'Oh yes, very good thank you. I do believe you may have a leaking roof. Woke up with a wet face. You should get it checked before the worst of the weather sets in.'

With that, he stumbled his way down the stairs and out into the street.

61

Ida was really not sure what to think about the bizarre and curious erotic refreshments on offer after the doors officially closed at Divine. As far as she was concerned, at that moment in time in her fledgling life, the after-hours sexual shenanigans only represented to her a means of gaining further financial independence.

Back in Marshcombe, when she was sweeping up at Mrs Noble's at a young age, she recalled hearing the local doctor's wife saying to Mrs Noble, 'My niece Patsy is doing ever so well for herself, really getting on in life. She is a nurse at Leicester Hospital.'

This one sentence had stuck with Ida. Even back then, she knew she wanted her own "get on in life" event and definitely a nurse she would not be; she wouldn't like taking care of annoying sick people. But "get on" she would, doing it her way and if fellating sweaty, wealthy gents was her way so be it.

Since arriving in Birmingham, she had only fleetingly thought of Sylvie. The first time was when Janice had taken her to the cinema. As they took their seats and settled in, Janice said, 'Your mum wanted to be in the flics.' Janice could have poked herself in the eye with a sharpened pencil for being so loose-tongued. She had promised herself never to talk of Sylvie in front of Ida unless Ida brought the subject of her mother up. Ida had not responded, only opened a small red and white striped paper bag and popped a lemon sherbet into her mouth without offering Janice a sweet.

On another occasion, she had walked past a cake shop and noticed iced buns, orderly placed in neat rows like white tombstones on a baking rack. She remembered Maude buying her one in Dingley and telling her how much her mother had loved them. Saying that Sylvie had always licked the white icing off the top of the bun before scoffing the rest.

62

Mrs Pritchard, as sharp-eyed as ever, had become very aware of how late Ida returned some evenings, usually mid-week, which intrigued her as she knew Ida worked in the fancy shop on Forde Street as a sales assistant and the shop closed at five o'clock. What made her ponder was that surely, they were not stock-taking that many evenings a month.

However, Mrs Pritchard assuaged her mild concern with the thought that Ida was a good tenant, clean and tidy but best of all her rent book was fully up to date. She had had a few qualms when Janice had moved on to get married. Pressing Janice for assurances that Ida was not "a messer" or a little slut. Janice had reassured her saying that she could vouch for Ida, that she had known her all her life and that she was raised by good Quaker folk.

Mrs Pritchard had responded by saying, 'I will not tolerate any nonsense as you well know Janice.' Both Ida and Janice had been somewhat creative regarding Ida's age.

Ida was very conscious that Mrs Pritchard had become aware of her arriving back late. One night as she had slid the key in the front door as sneakily as she possibly could, she had heard her landlady release an extremely loud sneeze, which appeared to come from Mrs Pritchard's keyhole, just to the right of the front door.

Ida had eased the front door closed and laughed all the way up the stairs to her tawdry room. She had already been thinking about moving once the evening "tricks" had accumulated her a tidy nest egg. Until then, she would be as quiet as a slumbering hedgehog and avoid her landlady as much as possible to avoid any awkward questions.

63

For two days now and quite unlike Marjorie, she had not been seen at Divine's. This was a rare occurrence as, unless she was away on a buying trip for stock, Marjorie always showed up at the shop although admittedly it could be noon before the girls set eyes on her. But this absence was due to the emotional upheaval caused by her precious Pico having succumbed to pancreatitis despite the heroic interventions of a vet.

However, on the third day after Pico's demise, Marjorie stormed into the showroom, which was luckily devoid of customers, demanding to inspect the girls. Immediately finding fault with Peggy's chipped thumbnail polish and Ida's hair.

'Where is Eunice?' she crowed.

'Upstairs having a lie-down, she has a headache,' Martha offered quietly. With that, Marjorie swivelled round as efficiently as a spinning top and made her way up the stairs, her heels clacking as she went, leaving the girls raising their eyebrows to the top of their foreheads in unison.

Marjorie pushed open the door of the big bedroom with such force that it knocked into the towel rail stand making it rock momentarily and barking at Eunice, 'Get up, my girl. This place is not a doss house as you well know.'

'Mother, I thought you were staying home today.'

'Clearly, that is what you thought Eunice. Now get up, ready yourself and go about making us prosper further.'

Rather sluggishly Eunice replied, 'Yes, yes, Mother, I will do.'

'Good. Please get Ida to bring me a tray of tea and some of those vanilla biscuits to the salon. I want you to make sure that those girls are lemon douching regularly. When I went past the kitchen just now, I noticed that the lemons were in exactly the same formation in the basket as they were two days ago. Clearly, they have not been following my high standards and expectations. You better tell them not to take me for a fool.'

Eunice slipped past her mother in the bedroom doorway. She longed to start her own "French polishing" business, particularly on days like these.

Her mother really was very tiresome at times she thought as she reapplied the Spring Kiss Pink lipstick in the bathroom mirror. But then none of the fine things Eunice so enjoyed as a young girl would have been possible if it had not been for her mother's tenacity, hard graft and tolerance for staring at ceilings.

Back down in the showroom where Peggy and Dina were engrossed with two buxom middle-aged women looking to purchase theatre outfits, Eunice gathered Lucy, Martha and Ida in the stock room.

'Girls, you need to look sharpish today. Mother is "doing one" and she is cross as hell about almost everything. Pico dying has set her in a right grumpy mood. She is particularly annoyed as she is of the belief that we have not been lemon douching quite as often as she would like. So please make sure you make amends and also tell Peggy and Dina when they are finished sticking dresses into those two. Ida, please take my mother a tray of tea and some vanilla biscuits up to the salon.'

Ida took the pot of tea and biscuits into Marjorie not before stuffing two of the scrumptious biscuits into her mouth and making sure she was devoid of evidence!

'Thank you, Ida. How are you today?' Marjorie asked stiffly but with a tone which belied the mood Ida had just witnessed downstairs.

Ida thought she was definitely after something.

'Very good…thank you. I am sorry to hear about Pico.' She braved.

'Yes, very sad, and I was so fond of him, and Dorothy is beside herself as she doted on that dog,' Marjorie said as she poured herself a cup of tea adding a dash of milk. And then she continued, 'Have you met Ernest Hemple the tall dark-haired man?'

'I have seen him but not spoken to him.'

'Well, he will be in this evening, and he would like to spend some time with you Ida. He is an important client so be your most obliging self.'

'Of course, Mrs Peyton. Thank you. I will.'

64

Six o'clock arrived and the girls, having freshened up, awaited the arrival of the gentlemen guests. Ida had quizzed Peggy and Martha about Ernest. Learning that he had plenty of money and was a successful commercial landlord. As with all the men, he too had a nickname, his being "Lickety-spit". Owing to his penchant for a vigorous blow job or as Lucy called it a snobberry goblin!

The salon gradually grew noisy with lively chatter and the clink, clink of glasses. Dina was doing a roaring trade in drinks and cocktails, having not heeded a single word of Marjorie's remonstration about overdoing the drinks.

Two men arrived that Ida had not seen before. Jeffrey Dedcott was a tall broad-shouldered man in his early fifties and very keen on a bow tie. He was the Midlands area National Schools Inspector and held no particular sexual predilection other than he occasionally enjoyed timing himself! Jeffrey had no sense of humour and very little in the way of conversation. The girls categorised him as "an easy".

The other man was Dr William Spigot who ran the orthopaedic department at the General Hospital. The girls found him amusing with his tales of the nurses' antics with some of his junior colleagues. When he was ready to go to one of the bedrooms, he would say, 'Come on Peggy it is high time I gave you a thorough examination!' It had been mildly amusing the first time he said it but as he said it every time he visited Divine, which was at least once a week, the joke had become rather stale.

Marjorie, whose mood had improved slightly as the day wore on, was somewhat irked as Ernest Hemple did not make an appearance that night. *Well*, she thought, *he doesn't know what he is missing*!

Ida was not in the least concerned at the nonappearance of Mr Hemple as she was kept busy with wrestling Sidney Simcox into his rabbit suit and feeding him carrots before he hopped onto Lucy! Ida thought she would never be able to look at carrots in a stew in quite the same way again. She then chortled to herself remembering Rose attacking home-grown earth-covered carrots with a blunt vegetable knife before hurling them into a saucepan.

65

Ida had not been in the least bit bothered that Ernest Hemple had failed to materialise that evening at the salon. She was back at her digs by nine and happy at that.

Marjorie, on the other hand, was not so happy. Later that night as she lay in her sumptuous bed back at home, the more she thought about it, the more annoyed she became. She and the elusive Mr Hemple had spoken at some considerable length a few weeks earlier on the subject "of a nice fresh young thing" as he had lasciviously put it. Marjorie had leant forward touching him reassuringly on the forearm and said, 'I have just the girl for you, Ernest; she is right up your alley.'

She then proceeded to whet his appetite further by describing Ida as an "earthy minx". Ernest Hemple's response had been so fervent. She was therefore surprised and disappointed at his absence. However, she consoled herself with the thought that her sometime admirer would now have to dig very deep into his initial embossed calf skin wallet if he wanted to conquer Ida's fuchsia fortress.

On Wednesday evening, the following week, the girls were in full flow with a very busy salon at Divine. Bedroom doors opened and closed at pace. The girls much preferred a busy evening as it represented bountiful purses at the end of the night.

The city had been much quieter over the summer months. Some of Marjorie's more consistent clients took time away from their businesses to holiday with their families. But now Divine's regular gentlemen callers were back in full harness.

Ernest Hemple duly arrived at seven o'clock brandishing two bottles of Marjorie's most favourite champagne. This olive branch guaranteed him an effusive greeting from Divine's matriarch. Well, at least to his face!

'Welcome, welcome, Ernest, how are you? We have not seen you in a while.'

'I am very well, and dandy thank you, Marjorie. As I am sure you are well aware, sometimes work must take precedence over pleasure. Now please will you introduce me to your "Earthy" minx.'

Marjorie beckoned over to Ida, who was handing a drink to another new guest who owned a string of chemists in the city. This person's presence had prompted Dina to remark, 'Hope the new chemist fella is good for some recreational drugs!'

Ida sauntered slowly over to Ernest and Marjorie. Introductions complete, Ida fetched him a whisky sour, and they sat with knees almost touching on the cream couch.

'How are you enjoying the city, Ida?'

'Oh, well enough thank you. Birmingham is very different from my hometown which is a world away from here.'

The whisky sour made its way down Ernest's gullet at a rapid pace. His prominent Adam's apple bobbed alarmingly as the gulps of alcohol descended into his oesophagus.

Meanwhile, this interaction was surreptitiously observed by Marjorie and Eunice.

'Ahaa, the rabbit has seen the hare,' Eunice whispered into her mother's gold earring bedecked right ear.

Ida asked if he would like another drink or a "freshener" as she had been taught to say by Eunice.

'No, thank you, Ida my dear. I'm just going to have a word with Marjorie.'

With that, he got up from the couch and went to the far end of the salon. For several minutes, he appeared to be in earnest conversation with Marjorie. *Perhaps he has changed his mind*, she thought. He had appeared pleasant enough to her, and she felt that albeit with her limited experience, he would be ideal as her first solo "lie-down" client.

The negotiations over, Ernest Hemple returned to the couch.

'Right, Ida, why don't we find a free room?' As Ida led the way, he followed her into the middle bedroom. After shutting the door, Ida chirped enthusiastically, 'What would you like to do, Mr Hemple?'

This form of enquiry had also been drilled into her by Eunice.

'Please take your clothes off and tie up your hair with this ribbon,' he said, handing her a long length of red ribbon that he had produced from his jacket breast pocket. Ida followed his instructions and then sat on the bed.

'Lie back on the pillows with your legs apart,' Ernest asked her.

She manoeuvred herself into the desired position with one swift movement of her svelte body.

As Ernest slowly and meticulously removed his suit jacket, waistcoat, tie, shirt, trousers, shoes and socks and finally his undershorts and placed them on a small green button-backed chair he never took his eye off the object of his lust. He approached the bed and spoke quietly, 'Now, sit in the middle of the bed with your back to me.'

He then knelt on the bed behind her and began stroking her breasts from over her shoulders. Ida felt his not-inconsiderable arousal pressing into the small of her back. He then pulled at the ribbon bow which held her luxuriantly thick hair aloft thereby releasing it onto her shoulders. Almost immediately he tied it up again before doing the same thing five more times.

This left Ida thinking that she wished he would get on with it as she was getting cold sat there.

After putting the ribbon back in her hair for the final time, he began to lick her left ear voraciously. Ida thought that this wet, large tongue was very much like a dog's, as it wiggled its way around the contours of her now very damp left ear. She found herself grinding her teeth by way of distraction, finding this particular form of foreplay ticklish and very, very annoying.

She wasn't self-conscious of her strangely odd left ear, but this was going on far too long. Suddenly he stopped, flipping the "earthy minx" and her slobbered ear onto her back. Ida hoped he was not going to attempt any further ear sex.

It was odd that none of the other girls had mentioned this peculiar predilection that Ernest Hemple was clearly so very keen on. She lay on the bed awaiting an instruction for oral sex, remembering what the others had told her. As she looked up at him, it occurred to her that if oral sex was about to be on the menu, her mouth might well not be ample enough.

This brought an inner giggle to her recalling how many times Jonjo said, 'What a gab you have on yer.'

As Ernest manoeuvred himself onto his elbows, it was now apparent to Ida what was required of her. Just as he was about to enter her, he said almost in a whisper, 'I had sex with a girl many years ago in a place called Marshcombe. Who bizarrely had the very same left ear as you, Ida…'

THE END